Hilary Rose is the pseudonym for Jane Heller, the *New York Times* and *USA Today* bestselling author of thirteen novels of romantic comedy, nine of which have sold to Hollywood for films and all of which have been entertaining readers around the world. She's also the author of two non-fiction books: a survival guide for caregivers and a humorous memoir about her passion for baseball.

A New York native and former book publicist, she currently makes her home in Santa Barbara, California, where she lives with her husband Michael, reads nonstop except when she's going to the movies, and is hard at work on her latest novel. And, of course, she continues to follow the trials and tribulations of the Forresters and the Logans and anybody else who shows up to create drama at Forrester Creations.

T0275541

Blindsided
by
Love

HILARY
ROSE

PAN
Pan Macmillan Australia

First published 2014 by Pan Macmillan Australia Pty Limited
1 Market Street, Sydney

978-1-250-07415-7

To my beloved Grandma Rose, who sat me on the floor of her apartment when I was a little girl, turned on the TV and watched her "stories." She converted me into a lifelong fan of daytime drama and I'll always be grateful.

Chapter One

This is so not working.

Caroline Spencer assessed her reflection in the full-length bedroom mirror and sighed with frustration, her vermilion-lacquered fingers splayed across her slim but shapely hips. At least the makeup was right—smoky shadow framing her brown eyes, iridescent highlighter emphasizing her cheekbones, peachy pink lipstick providing the needed color on her face. But her sun-kissed blond hair was swept up too tightly into the chignon her stylist had spent an hour constructing and her black V-neck dress plunged deeply enough to cause a wardrobe malfunction, and …

Bad dress plus bad hair equals hot mess.

She took off the offending garment and tossed it on the bed, which was already strewn with discarded outfits. So many clothes, so little time.

She needed to be at the restaurant opening by seven thirty and she was running more than fashionably late. Since when had she become so indecisive, so unsure of herself? Where was the spontaneous, impulsive, always-ready-to-party Caroline Spencer? The one who embraced challenges, the one who charged ahead without a backward glance? The one who was fearless?

Who are you and what have you done with Caroline?

She laughed ruefully at her reflection. The truth was that her divorce from Rick Forrester had flattened her, crushing her trademark exuberance. She could still fake the persona when she needed to, and she would—tonight, and all the other nights that were booked with galas and fundraisers and the see-and-be-seen events that were a staple of her social life in Manhattan. But she'd lost a piece of herself after Rick had betrayed her and she'd had no choice but to resign from Forrester Creations, his family's Los Angeles based fashion house best known for its elegant couture and youthful Hope for the Future lines. She couldn't stay there, not after her heart had been ripped to shreds, her pride left in tatters, and she'd decamped to New York six months ago. She had moved back into the turn-of-the-century townhouse on the city's posh Upper East Side where she'd spent most of her adult life, and though both her mothers traveled a lot, she had friends too, a genuine support system. She was still Caroline Spencer of Spencer Publications, the conglomerate her mom and Uncle Bill had turned into a publishing powerhouse. Her name carried significance, meant something around the world and allowed her to live very well, for which she was grateful. And yet she missed LA, missed designing for Forrester Creations, missed Rick. Maybe she didn't even miss Rick himself, not after what he'd put her through. And she certainly didn't miss the pain of his infidelity. What she yearned for was the kind of love they'd once shared. It had been so all consuming that she couldn't imagine not feeling it anymore, couldn't imagine feeling it again with someone new.

She flashed back to the brilliant sunny day when Rick had surprised her with a marriage proposal—on the curb outside Forrester Creations, the very spot where they'd first met. He'd gotten down on one knee, dazzling emerald-and-diamond engagement ring in hand, and said with a grin born of sheer joy, "From the very first moment I saw you, I knew I was going to be in trouble." They'd both laughed at the twisting, turbulent path their romance had taken. "With you is where I want to be," he'd continued with such certainty, so much adoration. "You never gave up on us. Spencer–Forrester is an unbeatable team to the end."

And they *were* a team in every way that mattered: his position as president of Forrester

Creations and her ability to carry out his vision for the company; his management skills and her creative designs; his ambition and drive and her "motor mouth," as he'd affectionately termed her tendency to shoot from the lip. And, of course, there was never a question about their physical connection; when they made love, there was nobody else on the planet.

And yet for him, there *had* been somebody else: Maya. Always Maya, his fall back whenever his confidence needed bolstering, the woman he'd rescued from the streets by hiring her as a company spokesmodel, the damsel in distress he couldn't resist saving. Maya was like a drug to him, a way to blur the cold realities of his life.

Caroline shuddered with the memory of coming home early from work that fateful afternoon and finding them together—in her house, her *bed*. It was ugly and traumatic and terribly sad. And possibly avoidable. If the almighty Ridge Forrester hadn't anointed himself chairman as well as CEO of Forrester Creations, hadn't stripped Rick of the president's title and installed his son Thomas there instead, hadn't debased and demeaned Rick at every opportunity, maybe he wouldn't have sought refuge in Maya's arms.

Enough, Caroline. That ship has sailed.

There was no point in rehashing the maybes. She'd get over Rick. She was well on her way. But she'd never go back to Forrester Creations and work for Ridge. Not a chance. He'd offered to make her head designer, reporting directly to him, but she was right to decline. Sure, he was talented—a "design genius," they called him in the fashion industry—and she could have learned a lot from him, but pretentious? Arrogant? Entitled? Judgmental? Please. He gave new meaning to the words.

Caroline hurried over to her closet, reached for the body-hugging black cocktail dress with the sheer, lacy bodice and wriggled into it. The next fix was her hair. She enjoyed wearing it up, exposing the cancer survivor ribbon tattoo at the nape of her neck to honor her namesake, her aunt Caroline, who'd lost her battle with leukemia. But tonight called for a looser, less constrained style. She pulled out all the pins, gave her head a quick shake and let her golden curls cascade down her back.

Better. Much better.

She nodded approvingly, then stepped into her black stilettos and started toward the door before turning to her reflection one final time.

Hey, Caroline? You really need to stop talking to yourself like some crazy old cat lady.

✻

"There you are, fabulous as ever," said her friend Gigi, kissing her on both cheeks. It was opening night at Luc's and both women were on the

exclusive guest list for the cocktail party. The latest
venture from renowned Parisian chef Luc Bergeron,
Luc's was shaping up to be *the* restaurant for the
foodie set. If the venue itself was any indication,
it was well on its way, from the spectacular Art
Deco interior to the hundred-plus prominent New
Yorkers mingling and sipping champagne. "Ready
to do battle? I see lots of tasty morsels and I'm not
talking about the food."

Caroline had known Gigi Hollister since
they'd gone to the same private school as kids.
But while Caroline was trying to heal from the
anguish of her divorce, Gigi, model thin with
coal-black hair as short as a boy's, had already
shed three husbands by age 25 and was on the
prowl for another.

As a DJ pulsed electronica throughout the
cavernous space and white tuxedoed servers
passed hors d'oeuvres and flutes of Dom
Pérignon, Gigi took off in pursuit of a
distinguished-looking man old enough to be her
grandfather and Caroline moved through the
crowd alone. It didn't take long before she was
encircled by a quartet of eligibles, who were
attractive in an entirely forgettable way. She
swung into party-girl mode, as though on
autopilot. She threw her head back in laughter at
their jokes and summoned up amusing anecdotes
of her own then flashed her patented high-wattage
smile, and the time passed pleasantly enough.

She was trying to look riveted by the Wall Street hedge fund manager who was droning on and on about accrual swaps, currency overlays and flow derivatives, when she distractedly reached for another glass of bubbly, lost control of the stem and watched in utter humiliation as the glass slipped just enough for the champagne to splatter onto the black silk shirt of—

Ridge Forrester?

"What are you *doing*?" she blurted out before she could process his presence. "Sorry, I meant what are you doing here? In New York?" She hadn't expected to see him anywhere, much less in her town, on her turf. He was so out of context here, and she was thoroughly disoriented. He was California personified—even his appearance screamed West Coast. New Yorkers dressed up for lavish parties, but there he was, without a tie, without a shave, in blue jeans, of all things. He did have a certain appeal for those who liked the scruffy dark hair that curled to his shoulders, the equally dark stubble that was always threatening to become a goatee, the deep cleft in his chin that gave him the look of a chariot-driving, sandals-wearing hero of one of those Biblical movies. He definitely wasn't her type—Rick was clean cut, polished, impeccable, much more traditionally handsome—and yet she couldn't help noticing that every woman in the room was drooling at the sight of Ridge Forrester.

"A pleasure to see you too, Caroline," he said with a bow at the waist. "How rude of me to allow my chest to run into your champagne."

See that? Such an inflated idea of his own importance. She'd been clumsy with her glass, granted, and now he was mocking her. Fine. She would mock him back. "Did you and your chest fly all the way across the country to collide with my alcoholic beverage?"

He laughed. "Still feisty, I see." He was unable to keep his eyes from roaming her body even as she could see him trying to maintain eye contact. "Actually, I came tonight to celebrate with a friend."

"Why am I not surprised? Does this *Playboy* centerfold have a name?" Of course God's gift to womankind had brought a date.

Ridge didn't bother to squelch a smirk. "The centerfold is taking the night off, but Luc is an old friend from Paris. The opening is a big event for him and his wife."

Okay, she thought. *So I guessed wrong.* Ridge Forrester without a woman on his arm was inconceivable, but so was the fact that she was standing there talking to him. "I'm sure Luc's extremely honored that you came," she said, matching his sarcasm. She reached for another glass of champagne as a waiter passed, careful to hold onto it this time.

"You don't like me, I get that," Ridge said, after a sip of his own drink. "But I've always liked you, Caroline. You're a terrific designer and you've got this—I don't know—this *spark*. What I can't figure out is what you ever saw in Rick. The guy's bad news."

Old habits die hard, so Caroline leaped to her ex-husband's defense in spite of how he'd hurt her. "You crushed his self-esteem, Ridge. He was doing just fine before you came back to the company."

He placed a hand on her shoulder as if to focus her and she nearly flinched. Had he ever touched her before? Surely there'd been handshakes between them, maybe even a hug here and there, but this time the physical contact felt intimate for some reason and it threw her off balance.

"Caroline," he said gently, leaning in closer so she'd hear him over the music. "I'm sorry about what happened between you and Rick, but I wasn't responsible for it."

"You were always putting him down."

"You were always trying to bail him out."

"You didn't have to demote him and promote Thomas."

"For the record, my decision was purely professional. I thought Rick's ideas were ill-conceived. But contrary to popular belief, Forrester Creations is a democracy. If Rick wants back into the executive suite, he can earn his way. I'm open to that." He smiled, taking his hand off her. "Now, can we talk about you? Are you designing these days?"

"Yes, like mad," she lied. "I'm with a fashion house here—small but very cutting edge. I've never been busier or more engaged in my work." She hadn't gone on a single job interview since leaving Forrester Creations and it bothered her. She'd always worked, never wanted to live off her family's good fortune, wasn't one of those ladies who lunch, and yet the only designing she had done since she'd landed in New York was the occasional scribble on her sketchpad at home, in front of the television. Her work at Forrester Creations had been so fulfilling, so exciting—the tight deadlines, the collaborations with the models, seamstresses and promotion people, the adrenaline rush of the fashion shows. She'd embraced it all and the experience would be hard to replicate. But Ridge didn't need to know any of that.

"We miss you at Forrester," he said. "We all miss you around the office, Dad, Thomas, Hope—everybody."

Rick was conspicuously absent from that list. He was much too busy with Maya to miss her. "Thank you. It's nice of you to tell me." Maybe Ridge wasn't so bad after all.

A waiter came by carrying a plate dotted with elegant little puff pastries and announced, "With Luc's regards, Mr. Forrester: his signature gruyere gougère amuse-bouche."

Caroline arched an eyebrow at Ridge. "So you do know the chef personally." She picked up one of the pastries, swallowed it quickly and washed it down with a gulp of champagne. She hadn't eaten since breakfast and she was starving—or was she nervous? She ate fast when she was nervous.

Ridge laughed.

"What's so funny?" she said. Did she have cheese on her chin? Pastry between her teeth? Melted butter on the tip of her nose?

"You—your attitude toward this thing of beauty." He scooped up a gougère and held it against the light of the chandelier, as if he were examining an object d'art. "You ate it with all the appreciation of someone forced to swallow a pill, Caroline."

Oh, spare me your disapproval, she thought. So typical of the Ridge Forrester she knew and loathed. He still judged, still acted as if he were above it all. "And what, may I ask, is *your* attitude toward this cheese ball?"

He sampled his gougère, taking his time chewing it. "Simple but extraordinary. The mornay sauce adds to the richness of the cheese, the pastry is flaky and light, and the gruyere brings a slightly nutty note. Luc's creations tap into almost all the senses: smell, sight, feel and, of course, taste. Here, try another, only this time make it a memory."

Nutty is right. She'd heard that Ridge read poetry by famous English romanticists and often quoted from their sonnets, but apparently he was also an authority on the amuse-bouches of famous French chefs. "You're quite the wordsmith, aren't—"

Before Caroline could get another word in, Ridge picked up a gougère and popped it straight into her mouth, silencing her. He allowed his fingertips to trail across her lips; he couldn't take his eyes off them, she noticed.

"Good food is like good sex," he said, his voice husky and low, nearly a whisper, his face close to hers, "a sensual experience meant to be savored, not rushed."

If you say so, Caroline thought as the melted gruyere oozed down her throat. Ridge Forrester was a piece of work, with his lofty ideals and opinions. "Do you rhapsodize about food like this when you're eating a burger and fries?" she said. It was fun trying to take him down a peg even as she couldn't stop staring at that valley in his chin.

"Actually, I do, if they're top quality." He smiled. "Using all our senses … it's the key to enjoying life to the fullest."

"Interesting," she said. "I'll try to remember that as I make a—what was it you said? Oh, right, a *memory*." She scooped up another gougère, placed it on her tongue and let it roll around in her mouth before swallowing it. "I'm sensing just a hint of leeks. Or is it fennel? I get the two mixed up. Either way, I'm experiencing an infusion of both the savory and the sweet, a melding of the yin and yang, the masculine and the feminine, the balance of the universe. The aroma is like a cloud of French perfume that wafts and floats and—"

"All right, all right." He laughed, his face relaxing into a wide grin. "I know when I'm being parodied." He reached for her hand and held it. "I should go find Luc and congratulate him, since he's the reason I'm here."

"Yes, of course you should."

"Seeing you again has been ... entertaining," he said. "If you ever change your mind and want a job at Forrester Creations, you know where I am. But the small, cutting-edge fashion house you mentioned has you under contract, yes? What was the name of it again?"

The name of it. *Great, Caroline. Now what? Come up with something—fast.* "Luna Designs," she ventured, pulling a word out of the air, thinking she'd be more suited to a company called Lunatic Designs. "Small but growing." It was nice of him to offer her a job and they'd had a fairly pleasant exchange just now, but it was quite another to actually work for him. Not happening.

"Well, then ... Best of luck with it and be well, Caroline." Only then did he release her hand and turn to go.

As soon as he had disappeared into the sea of revelers, Gigi scurried over, breathless and a bit tipsy, judging by her flushed cheeks and ragged gait. "Tell me, tell me."

"Tell you what?"

"How I can get Ridge Forrester to play hand-sies with me like that." She licked her lips. "Now he's my idea of hot."

Caroline wrapped her arm around her friend's shoulder and gave her a squeeze. "Gigi, you thought the geezer with the ascot and the turkey neck was hot."

"Oh, stop. So Ridge is Rick's older brother?"

"Half-brother, sort of. Complicated family history there." Her mind did a quick replay of their interaction. "He was pretty chatty tonight, I'll give him that," she said. "He's usually a man of few words—the silent, brooding, Heathcliff-on-the-moors type. He offered me a job again, by the way."

"He's a catch, Caroline. If he offered me a job, I'd be on it in six seconds."

"I'm not going back to Forrester Creations," Caroline said firmly. "Not in this lifetime anyway."

Chapter Two

"Any questions? Concerns?" Ridge asked the Forrester Creations team seated around the conference table in his opulently furnished, wood-paneled office, which was twice the size of most people's living rooms and adorned with display cases chock full of fashion industry award statuettes. "If not, I've got work to do this afternoon. We all do."

He didn't wait for an answer but instead rose from the table, strode purposefully to his desk, picked up his sketchpad and sat down with a determined sigh—a clear signal to everybody that the meeting was adjourned. Hope, Rick, Donna and Pam all filed out. Only Thomas stayed behind.

A younger, rangier, fresh-faced version of his father, Thomas had three qualities Ridge valued most in his new president and second-in-command: talent, ambition and loyalty. He and Thomas didn't butt heads—they were in sync about the company's direction. There was none of the testiness Ridge had had to put up with in his conversations with Rick. And he enjoyed watching his son grow into the job. Ever since his own father, the legendary Eric Forrester, had decided to spend more time traveling than running Forrester Creations—not a retirement, Eric was emphatic in pointing out, just a stepping back from the day-to-day operations—Ridge had relied on Thomas to help carry out his vision. Thomas was bright and eager to learn how to run the business, leaving Ridge to design and oversee the couture line on which Forrester Creations had built its reputation for class and elegance. As for the ever-resentful Rick, he was the point man on his sister's Hope for the Future line. He also looked after Brooke's Bedroom, the lingerie division his mother had conceived, while Brooke spent most of her time sharing custody of RJ and deciding where else she wanted to put her energy these days—and with whom. There no longer a "Brooke and Ridge" and hadn't been in well over a year. While Ridge felt the loss of the connection they'd shared—a connection that had lasted for what seemed like an eternity—and he would always love her, the way you always love your most enduring romantic partner, he was relieved to be free of the constant drama that had been the hallmark of their relationship. Now they were cordial with each other, active co-parents to RJ, and that would suffice. He was intent on protecting his ten-year-old son from unnecessary drama and upheaval, and so far he'd been successful. The boy was happy, well adjusted and safe. Perhaps he would campaign for RJ to join the family business someday, perhaps not. In the meantime, he hoped to convey to his son his love of the artistry of designing.

"Seems like all the details for the fundraiser are coming together," said Thomas. "Donna has the ballroom booked and the invitations are mailed, and Pam is working with the event planner on flowers, seating, catering—"

"Wait," said Ridge, looking up from his pad, his hand raised like a school crossing guard. "Catering? Please tell me you mean Pam's made contact with Luc Bergeron's people, not that she thinks she's cooking for two hundred guests. We're talking about high rollers who won't be satisfied with her pot roast and lemon bars."

They shared a chuckle. "No worries, Dad," said Thomas. "She gets it. Your buddy Luc's on the case."

Ridge's aunt Pam had a kind heart and enjoyed feeding anybody and everybody, but the fashion show and dinner to honor the anniversary of Stephanie Forrester's death and raise money for cancer research required the best chef in town. Ridge still regretted that he hadn't come home to LA to be with his mother during her final days. It had been her wish that he remain in Paris, that he not see her in pain, not witness her dying, and he'd respected it, but the decision haunted him. She'd been such a force of nature, such a dominant presence in his life, and he missed her. She was the Forrester matriarch and it was surreal that she wasn't around to set the agenda, champion causes and twist arms when necessary.

"Grandmother wouldn't want to miss an event like this," said Thomas wistfully.

"She would have run the show top to bottom." Ridge glanced at the silver-framed photo of his mother that sat on his desk next to the one of RJ, sporting his yellow soccer uniform. "But it sounds like we're moving forward with it."

"All that's left to do is design the gowns and fit the models," said Thomas. "And that's in your wheelhouse, Dad."

Ridge nodded. The "fashion" part of the fashion show fundraiser rested on his shoulders and he felt the pressure. The event was only three months away and while he'd already drawn a number of sketches that satisfied him, it was a complicated process from sketchpad to runway. He needed to bring his concepts to life, see them on the models, feel the fabrics, hear the feedback from his team. Time to step it up.

"You'll make it happen," Thomas said, giving his father a loving pat on the shoulder. "You always do. And we'll raise thousands to honor Grandmother."

Ridge smiled, grateful for his son's support.

His cell phone rang: Brooke. He noticed with a bittersweet pang that his heart no longer thumped in his chest at the sight of her name on his caller ID now their conversations were usually about RJ's welfare: his schoolwork, athletic activities and custodial visits. Very different from the old days, when their lives revolved around their next romantic escapade.

"What's up, Brooke?" he said while Thomas checked his own phone for messages.

She was agitated—incoherent, hurried, her words flooded with emotion—on top of which her cell signal was breaking up and she kept getting cut off.

"Slowly. I can't understand you," he said, suddenly on high alert, knowing it wasn't like her to break down without good reason.

"Heard on the news ... wildfire in Malibu Canyon ... Los Padres National Forest ... RJ's ..."

Ridge felt his whole body go rigid. "He's what?"

"At his friend Kyle Hanson's ... Lives nearby ... Kyle's parents are at work ... I'm in San Diego ... Can't get back in time, but RJ ..."

"Could be in big trouble," he said, his voice rising, his pulse quickening. His son, their son, was staying at the Hansons'. Depending on where the fire was and in which direction it was moving, RJ could indeed be in grave danger. "I'm on my way."

*

Ridge drove like a man on a mission. As he headed down toward the Pacific Coast Highway, he was glued to the local radio station that provided periodic news updates. For years, Malibu had been prone to wildfires, backing up to the vast Los Padres National Forest as it did, and California had been grappling with a record-breaking drought combined with high temperatures, low humidity and brittle brush, leaving the state a veritable tinderbox. With howling Santa Ana winds whipping through the canyons, especially in the afternoons and after sundown, conditions were ripe for disaster and firefighters were stretched, their resources at an all-time low.

"The Malibu fire, newly designated the Rancho Fire, remains at just under five thousand acres, but it's early going with zero containment," said the news announcer. "The raging blaze has destroyed a dozen structures in a rural area. So far it's keeping its distance from the major housing developments. But it's all about the wind direction, folks. We're asking the public to be very aware. This is a dangerous, rapidly moving fire. If you are asked by fire officials to evacuate, leave now and remember you will not be allowed back in. If you're under a voluntary evacuation warning, you're not required to leave but it would be wise to do so, as conditions can change quickly."

The announcer went on to list the neighborhoods that were under a mandatory evacuation order and those that were still under a warning only. Kyle's house was in the warning area, a good ten miles away from the blaze, but that was small comfort. All Ridge cared about was RJ, getting to him, making sure he was safe, taking no chances by bringing him home.

Once he reached the Pacific Coast Highway, there was no mistaking the thick, sulfurous layers of smoke off in the distance, up in the hills, away from the ocean—acrid white-gray billows that indicated the inevitable scarlet flames engulfing everything in their path.

Hurry, he prodded himself, trying to find a balance between driving responsibly and weaving in and out of heavy traffic. He'd tried to reach RJ on his cell phone numerous times but the boy didn't answer his texts or calls. He'd tried Kyle's family's landline but there was no response there either. *I'm coming, kid. I love you.*

At last Ridge made it to the turnoff that would take him up to Kyle's house. As he navigated the twisting, narrow canyon roads that snaked their way up to the Hansons' neighborhood, he could see flames loping over the top of the mountain and his heart dropped down to his knees. *It's still miles away*, he reminded himself. *They're not in the mandatory evacuation area. There's still time.*

The smoky air became oppressive, difficult to breathe. Ridge rolled up his car windows and turned on the air conditioner. He was a fashion designer not a firefighter, but he and Brooke had taken a public safety training course after RJ was born, so he knew the basics.

As he pulled into the Hansons' driveway, he was relieved not to find an inferno, but the feeling didn't last. A shower of ash rained down on him, trees and branches had fallen to the ground and stray embers licked at the shingle roof of the white wood-frame house. Had the wind direction changed? Was the fire growing closer and faster than predicted?

"RJ! Kyle!" he shouted as he pounded his fist on the front door, knowing they might not hear him; the ferocious wind was so loud it muffled all other sounds. "Open the door!"

Nothing. He couldn't just stand there like a guest at a party. He had to do something, take action. In one swift motion, he picked up a sizable downed branch and hurled it against a window, shattering it, and climbed inside the living room, threading himself through the shards of broken glass and cutting the skin on his forearms in the process.

"Dad!" RJ flung himself into his father's chest the instant he entered the house, while Kyle grabbed Ridge from behind. They were both scared, that much was obvious, but otherwise unhurt, Ridge could see. "We were playing video games out by the pool and didn't know anything was wrong until we saw the smoke. Kyle said we would have gotten a reverse 911 call if we were supposed to get out." He spoke so rapidly his words ran together and he kept coughing, his throat clogging from the smoke that had become unbearable, but he was trying to put on a brave face.

"It's okay. But we'll leave now just to be safe, since Kyle's parents are probably stuck in traffic trying to get here and we'd better not wait for them." Ridge turned to RJ's friend, a skinny ten-year-old with red hair and freckles. "Do you have any bandanas, Kyle? And could you run and get them so we can all breathe easier—quickly?" He tried to keep his demeanor calm so as not to frighten the boys and betray his own sense of urgency, but time was of the essence, mandatory evacuation or not.

Kyle nodded tremulously.

While he hurried off to his bedroom, Ridge checked the Hansons' landline to try to call the fire department, but there was no dial tone. Chances were that power lines in the area were down along with the phone lines. Kyle returned with a handful of bandanas, his cheeks flushed with anxiety, and Ridge tied the red and blue kerchiefs over the boys' faces as fast as his fingers could move, covering their noses and mouths before fastening his own.

"Let's go, boys," he said, taking each of them by the hand. "We need to get out of here, quick."

As they exited through the front door, Ridge could hear the faintest sound of sirens against the roar of the gusty winds, the crackling of ever-encroaching flames and the sizzling of the occasional ember against the house's wood-shake roof. *Good news, bad news*, he thought as they stepped gingerly toward his waiting car, careful not to trip on branches or debris. Good news that the engines were on their way. Bad news that the wind must have shifted in their direction. *How fast things can change*, he thought yet again, well aware of past fires and their unpredictable turns.

After he loaded the boys into the back seat of the car and buckled them in, he raced to the house's front door to make sure he'd left it unlocked in case the fire crews needed easy access.

He was only yards away from reaching for the door's brass handle when the roof, which had been dusted by what had seemed to be only a few itinerant embers, burst into flames, caving in and collapsing as dramatically as if there had been a demolition. Time froze as a huge, swirling, night-marish orb of orange swallowed the entire house.

Ridge was thrown to the ground by the force of the fireball, its boom as thunderous as an explosion, like a grenade detonating.

"Dad!" RJ cried. "I'm coming to—"

"Stay in that car!" Ridge shouted, his head in his hands, the blast echoing in his ears, reverberating throughout his body.. "And look away from the house! Both of you!"

"But you're—"

"I'm okay, I'm okay," said Ridge. He could feel the lacerations on his face through the now-shredded bandana, but they were just superficial cuts. And the weakness and shakiness in his limbs would pass, he knew. It was his eyes ... They were burning as if they had caught fire along with the house. Ridge's eyes felt seared, charred by the intense light of the flames he'd witnessed at close range. He blinked his lids closed and then opened them again and when he did he saw nothing but darkness, like in the moment after a flash photograph.

I can't see, he thought with a terrifying jolt. *My God, I can't see!*

He didn't have a moment to waste. Surely the darkness would clear and he'd be able to get in the car and drive the boys to safety, wouldn't he? As he staggered to his feet he blinked again and again, giving his vision another chance to right itself. It did, but only barely. When he closed and opened his eyes, he saw what looked like a spider web of cracks and very blurry images and shadows. Not good enough to navigate narrow roads that were likely to be strewn with debris and downed power lines. Still, maybe if his son could direct him, point out obstacles in their path, he could do it. He had to do it.

Somehow he managed to reach the car. "RJ, Kyle, help me into the driver's seat, okay?"

He could hear Kyle sniffing and assumed the boy was in tears. It was his family's house that was ablaze, after all. And both boys were coughing, having inhaled so much smoke. But they each took one of Ridge's arms and guided him into the driver's seat, then strapped themselves back in.

Ridge quickly realized with a sinking feeling that it would be foolhardy to try to drive with vision that was so severely impaired. He didn't want to be responsible for making an already horrendous situation worse. He needed help, divine or otherwise, and fast.

Desperate, nearly out of his mind with the burning in his eyes and his concern for the boys, he envisioned his mother, seized on the image of the formidable Stephanie Forrester looking down on them with her all-knowing expression, the one she bore in the oil painting that still hung over his father's living room fireplace. He pictured her taking charge now, in this crucial moment, making it her business to ensure their safety.

Come on, Mom. I've done the best I can. Now it's your turn.

Suddenly, there was the rumbling of trucks and voices and then the sound of heavy tires crunching against the gravel driveway.

Footsteps came next, and a blur of figures approached the car.

"Sir? We need you to let us take it from here."

Ridge couldn't see them clearly, but he could certainly hear the strike team's commands to him and the boys, sense the firefighters' firm, gloved hands lifting all of them into an SUV.

*

Many, many hours later, after a procession of doctors at the hospital had asked Ridge questions, poked needles into his veins and sent him for a battery of tests, family members gathered around his bed, two at a time. They reassured him that RJ and Kyle were fine, that they'd been treated and released. And they kept calling him a hero, heralding his bravery and courage and every other laudatory adjective in the dictionary, but Ridge shook his head over and over and made it clear that the pros were the ones who had shepherded them all to safety. He didn't mention his mother's part in the rescue; that was his secret. And his family didn't mention the white bandages that blanketed his eyes and made it impossible for him to see even a shadowy glimpse of them.

RJ's safe, thought Ridge as he slid into the haze of the medications the nurse had administered. *My boy is safe.*

Just before he slept, he reached up to touch his eyes and felt the bandages. "I have a fashion show to …" he slurred to the nurse who stood over his bed, adjusting its angle so he could rest more comfortably. "Will my vision come back in time … ?"

He didn't finish his question, and the nurse didn't answer it.

Chapter Three

"Great to hear from you," Caroline said, checking her watch. It was not only early for Hope Logan to be calling—seven a.m. in LA—but they hadn't spoken in quite a while; since Caroline had left for New York, they'd kept in touch only sporadically. Not because they hadn't been close—they'd been caring sisters-in-law who'd worked together seamlessly at Forrester Creations, shared confidences and had Rick's best interests at heart. But recently Hope had kept her distance, sensitive to the fact that Caroline was trying to heal from her breakup with Rick and that constant calls and texts from her would only bring back painful memories. And she was right. After Caroline had seen Ridge at the restaurant opening a few months ago, the old wounds had flared and gnawed at her. She'd spent days after their chance meeting reliving the shock of finding Rick and Maya together, analyzing every conceivable way she could have prevented their affair. And running into Ridge had only ramped up her ill will toward him for stripping Rick of the president's title and setting in motion the collapse of her marriage, however inadvertently. But she'd emerged from her gloom and doom, and on this crisp autumn morning in Manhattan, she was having a late breakfast with Gigi and feeling pretty good about life. She'd even interviewed with a fashion design house, Leigh Nixon Designs; a competitor of Forrester Creations in the couture market, in fact. She had no idea if she'd get the job, but it was heartening that they'd liked her work enough to schedule a second interview.

"What's got you up so bright and early today?" she asked Hope.

"The fashion show and cancer fundraiser we're pulling together—or trying to," she said, sounding stressed, her voice more plaintive than conversational. "It's to commemorate the anniversary of Stephanie's death and it's less than two months away, and I didn't know who else to talk to about it."

"I'm glad you came to me." Caroline naturally assumed Hope was reaching out to her because of the Caroline Spencer Cancer Foundation, the research fund she'd set up to honor her aunt Caroline and which had raised money at countless fundraisers in New York. "Happy to share my experience, so whatever you need: donors mailing lists, tips on raffle tickets, ways to run blind auctions, all of it."

"'Blind' being the operative word," said Hope with a heavy sigh.

"Sorry, I don't understand." Caroline shrugged her shoulders at Gigi, who was sitting across the table, glued to her friend's side of the conversation as she picked at her fruit and granola.

"Okay, here it is." Hope heaved another sigh, one that foreshadowed something serious or upsetting or both. "I called about the fundraiser, yes, but I'm more worried about the fashion show. We all are."

Caroline smiled, remembering how much pressure accompanied the shows at Forrester Creations, how every countdown to show time was fraught with last-minute complications and snafus and how the adrenaline rush of it all was just the sort of high-energy problem-solving she thrived on. "It'll get done and it'll be a huge success," she reassured Hope. "You'll see."

"Not this time, Caroline. There's a problem. I've been beating around the bush and I apologize, but I didn't know how—we've kept the situation out of the media."

"The media? If that's what's worrying you, I make it a point not to read anything about Forrester Creations or the people who work there," said Caroline, not unkindly. "It's better for my mental health. And I don't gossip about the family, you know that. I've been trying to move forward with my life and I'm starting to."

"And I'm happy for you, but I need you—*we* need you—to come back."

"Come back to Forrester Creations? You've got to be kidding." Caroline laughed. She glanced over at Gigi and rolled her eyes. The very idea was insane.

"To help Ridge finish the designs for the show. It's in less than two months, as I said, and there's no other designer who understands the company like you do, who tackles challenges like you do. I know, I know. You were the lead designer on Hope for the Future, not couture, but you wear Ridge's designs all the time, Caroline. You're practically a runway model for the line."

"You had me at 'Ridge,' Hope," she said, reeling from the entreaty that seemed to come out of the blue. She took a sip of her latte and tried to recover her bearings. "I'm flattered that you think I could work on his line, but you know I'm not exactly his biggest fan. Why isn't he asking me himself, by the way?"

"He'd never ask. He's much too proud to ask you or anyone else for help."

"One of his many wonderful character traits: overweening pride." Caroline sighed. "But why does he even need help? He's the chairman and

CEO now. He's been designing for Forrester Creations' fashion shows for years. He can do it with his eyes closed."

Hope cleared her throat, as if preparing to drop a bombshell—and she did. "It's his eyes that are the problem. He's blind, Caroline," she said finally, tentatively. "For all intents and purposes, Ridge is blind."

"What?" Caroline sat back in her chair and placed her hand on her heart, trying to steady herself. "Blind, as in stubborn, or blind, as in he can't see?" She had been with Ridge only a few months ago and he'd looked perfectly healthy.

"There was a wildfire in Malibu—you probably read about that part—and Ridge was there. He suffered what doctors say is a form of ocular trauma called flash blindness. It happens a lot to soldiers in combat if they're exposed to IEDs. Ridge's case is a much milder version. Not to get too clinical about it, but basically the extremely intense light from the fire burned his retinal cells. The condition is usually temporary, but the retinal pigment hasn't regenerated and the vision impairment has lasted longer than anybody expected."

"Oh my God. I can't believe this." Caroline pushed her plate of eggs and toast away, having suddenly lost her appetite. She felt numb, tried to make sense of Hope's shocking news, tried to picture what Ridge must be going through.

For all his faults, he was so vital, so larger-than-life, the standard bearer of Forrester Creations. To imagine him having to deal with this sudden loss of vision, to imagine him losing the ability to design and run the show and do what he loved, to imagine him reduced or vulnerable or any less than Superman, was inconceivable. "I'm so sorry. What was Ridge doing in Malibu to begin with?"

Hope filled her in on Ridge's daring rescue of RJ and his friend Kyle, their own rescue by the LA County Fire Department, the harrowing trip to the emergency room, the diagnosis of his condition and its aftermath: the spots, the shadows, the blurry images, the residual pain, along with the dark moods, angry outbursts and constant frustration of having to wear sunglasses, keep away from all light sources, of not being fully functional at the office or anywhere else for that matter. "It's not that he can't see at all," she said. "It's that he can't see well enough to finish the designs for the fashion show, and he's more withdrawn, more into his own head. He's just not the same."

"I'm so, so sorry," Caroline repeated as she tried to process all the information Hope had related. No, she wasn't Ridge's biggest fan, but she'd never wish him harm. She'd never wish any of them harm—not even Maya. "I can't believe I didn't hear about this before."

"We really have tried to keep it private—for many reasons. But now we've got the show weighing on everybody."

"Have you thought about canceling it, or at least postponing it until Ridge recovers?"

"He won't hear of it. He says it's about Stephanie, about honoring her legacy, plus he's in denial, Caroline. He's deluded himself into believing that the distorted images he sees on his sketchpad will somehow translate into beautiful dresses. But he can't execute his designs alone, that's the sad truth, and there's nobody else who can pick up the slack, be his eyes, implement his concepts. Thomas's design expertise is menswear, and he's got his hands full trying to help run the business right now. Eric would love to pitch in, but he's had recent health issues of his own—a heart problem that put him in the hospital and gave us all a scare—and he's supposed to take it easy, which means keeping him away from the office. And Rick, well, he's not a designer, as you know all too well."

Caroline inhaled deeply, her head spinning. Poor Gigi was sitting across the table wondering what was going on. She kept mouthing the words "Tell me," but there would be plenty of time to talk. Now was the time to listen.

"You'd only have to stay until the fundraiser's over," Hope went on. "Just to work with Ridge on the designs. Believe it or not, he didn't hate the idea of you helping him. You're the only name on our list he didn't reject."

"I guess I'm flattered," said Caroline.

"You should be. You could take Steffy's office," said Hope, referring to Ridge's daughter. "She's still in Paris so it's sitting there empty and you'd have it all to yourself. Now, I want to be clear: you don't have to commit to anything beyond the fashion show, I promise. We'd fly you in on the Forrester jet, set you up with a limo and driver, put you up at a hotel—whatever you need while you're in LA."

I used to live in the Forrester guest house with Rick, Caroline thought, blinking back the memories of both the happy times there and their anguished final days.

"And then there's Rick," Hope added as if reading Caroline's mind. "He's done with Maya—for good this time. She doesn't work at Forrester Creations anymore. She's not even in town, as far as I know. But more importantly, he's dying for you to come back, Caroline. He agreed to let me be the one to approach you, but he'd do anything to make things right between you, he really would. He still loves you and he's beating himself up for what happened between you. Won't you at least give him another chance while you're here?"

"I haven't said I'm coming, Hope."

Rick still loved her? Wanted to make things right between them? Hope had delivered another bombshell and Caroline had to admit that her heart did a little dance when she heard the words, but was it even possible for Rick to make things right? He had a history with Maya, just as he had a history with her. He'd strayed with Maya before they were even married, for God's sake.

And yet he'd not only come back to her, but proposed to her and married her at an impromptu wedding on Thanksgiving Day in front of close friends and family.

You have taken me on some wild rides and I've jumped off a few times, but I always came back.

That's what he'd said when he'd gotten down on one knee and proposed to her. He always came back. The question was, could she be open to his coming back this time? Could she ever trust him again? Could she ever let herself love him again?

And there was Ridge. The idea of working with him when he was fully capable was unappealing enough, but now? With his impaired vision and those dark moods and angry outbursts Hope had mentioned, wouldn't he be even more difficult, more demanding, more judgmental? Caroline was no scared little mouse and she could stand up to anybody, but she'd never had to deal with a man as obstinate and entitled as he was—in his condition and under a tight deadline, no less.

Still, she was a compassionate person—being around cancer patients had taught her so much about empathy and gratitude—and she did feel for him, for his suffering and for the family's predicament over how to handle it. He could be kind and gentle when he wanted to be—she'd seen it—and designing for the couture line at Forrester Creations would be incredibly satisfying for her, as well as career defining.

And there was Terry Jarvis, the man who didn't just teach her about dealing with obstacles but schooled her in what it meant to tackle them head on.

She hardly ever talked about it, about Terry, but she couldn't help thinking of him now, of how they met years ago when she'd first established her foundation and he'd served as a board member. She was young and impetuous and he was older and wiser—and ill with brain cancer, though in remission and functioning at a high level. A former musician who'd landed in the recording industry and risen to the position of VP at one of the major record labels, he was in the prime of his life, riding high, traveling the world with the music industry's best-known artists. He was charming and charismatic and sexy, and Caroline had fallen for him. They weren't together long before his cancer came back—with a vengeance. Still, she never wavered in her feelings for him, even knowing that he was dying, even watching him lose his sight as a result of the tumor, and he never wavered in his courage or his joy for living, not until he took his last breath.

Knowing him, however briefly, had transformed her from a frivolous girl into a woman with more depth of character than a lot of people gave her credit for.

"Caroline? Will you do this for us?" Hope pleaded, bringing her back to the present and the situation at hand.

"You said Ridge is in denial. He doesn't even think he needs help."

"True, but he likes you. He respects you, respects your work. I'm not saying it would be easy—he'd resist your interference at first, no question. But you'll wear him down, if I know you." Hope allowed herself one of her little giggles that belied how strong and independent she'd become. "So will you do it? Say yes, please?"

Life can change in an instant, Caroline thought, as she continued to sit back in her chair and ponder the significance of Hope's phone call. She gazed across the table at her friend Gigi, who'd been a promising dancer with the New York City Ballet before her accident: she'd ruptured two discs in her neck after being hit by a speeding taxi while she was crossing Third Avenue.

Life can change in an instant.

The words echoed in her mind and resonated. One minute you're going along, thinking you have it all and the next minute you lose your eyesight in a wildfire, like Ridge, or you're diagnosed with brain cancer, like Terry, or your dreams of being a prima ballerina vanish because you go for a walk in your neighborhood, like Gigi. Personal tragedies were everywhere. What did it all mean? What was the message? *Was* there a message?

Yes, Caroline thought. There was. We have to live every moment to the fullest, not hold back, not hold onto fear and negativity and not obsess over every petty slight and past hurt. We can never predict what's coming and there's no way to prepare. So we need to just live. *Just live*—a cliché maybe, but it felt truthful to Caroline.

"I'll come," she told Hope, praying she was making the right decision, knowing it wasn't the safe one. "I'll make sure there are Forrester Creations designs on that runway on the big night—classic, elegant designs that'll be well worth the price of whatever you're charging for a fundraiser ticket. Designs your family can be proud of."

"Thank you. Thank you. Thank you." Hope squealed with delight and relief. "And Rick? Will you let him try to win you back?"

"I can't answer that one," she said. "It'll have to take care of itself."

After she and Hope hung up, Gigi, whose jaw had dropped midway through the conversation, said, "How soon am I losing you to the land of palm trees and boob implants?"

"Tomorrow morning," said Caroline. "It sounds like they really need me, like *yesterday*."

"So you're venturing back into that jungle of dysfunction," Gigi said, running her hand through her pixie haircut.

"I'll get to see my uncle," she said. "That's something positive."

"Bill Spencer." Gigi giggled. "Speaking of dysfunction. You staying with him?"

"God, no." She laughed. "He doesn't need his niece around. I'll camp out at a hotel, since it's a short-term assignment."

"Unless Rick convinces you to stay."

"I have no idea what'll happen with that. I'm going with zero expectations."

"One thing you know for sure," said Gigi. "Rick, the supposedly reformed ex-husband, and Ridge, the sight-challenged, high-maintenance designer, hate each other with the white-hot passion of a thousand burning suns—or whatever that expression is—and you'll be right smack in the middle of them. You've got guts, Caroline."

"Either that or I'm just plain crazy."

Chapter Four

True to her word, Hope had arranged for a limo to meet Caroline at LAX, drive her to Beverly Hills and remain at her disposal for the duration of her stay, which would be at the Beverly Wilshire Hotel, in a huge corner suite overlooking Rodeo Drive. A bottle of the finest California chardonnay chilling in a sterling silver ice bucket and a Baccarat crystal vase overflowing with roses, hydrangeas and dahlias welcomed her to her temporary home; Forrester Creations didn't do anything halfway: Caroline had to give them that. If the hotel was good enough for Richard Gere and Julia Roberts in *Pretty Woman*, it was good enough for her. She only wished her story could have the kind of happily ever after that the movie's lovers did.

She sighed as she looked at her mound of luggage. She never did learn how to pack economically, always cramming too many clothes into her bags "just in case." So silly. Not only were the shops of Rodeo Drive steps away, including the Forrester Creations boutique, but she'd be working for a prestigious fashion house with stock rooms full of anything and everything she could possibly want. But there wasn't time to scold herself for her indulgences or to unpack all those bags. She'd promised Hope she'd head straight over to the office, ease her way into Ridge's good graces and set her mission impossible in motion.

She gave herself a quick glance in the mirror, fluffed her hair, smoothed the skirt of her dress and straightened her spine. She looked the part of the confident professional but she was nervous about how Ridge would react to her being thrust on him. Would he accept her help? Approve of their collaboration? Appreciate that they had a job to do and a deadline in which to do it? And, of course, she was also nervous about how she would feel when she was face to face with Rick for the first time since their divorce. Would it sting to see him? Would he find a way to melt her heart? Did she want him to?

You can do this, Caroline. You're committed to doing this. Don't be a wuss.

She laughed as she realized she was talking to herself again, then grabbed her leather tote containing her tablet, designs and sketchpad and went to the lobby.

"Your car and driver are waiting, Ms Spencer," said the concierge as he opened the hotel's grand front door for her.

Caroline thanked him and walked toward the same black sedan that had fetched her at the airport, only to find not the uniformed driver, but Rick, in a dapper navy-blue suit, blue-and-white pinstriped shirt, navy tie and crisp white hand-kerchief tucked flawlessly in his breast pocket. His eyes were piercingly blue against the LA sky and his dark blond hair shone in the brilliant sunshine. He was so handsome that he bordered on beautiful—one of those impossibly high-cheek-boned, square-jawed comic-strip heroes who speak in little balloon captions. And he was holding something: a single sunflower, the very first thing he'd given her after they'd met. He'd told her it was her signature flower because it brightened any space with its cheery yellow petals and generous heart, just like she did. She assumed it was a peace offering.

And so it begins, she thought as she inhaled his familiar cologne, a subtle woody scent, and a wave of pleasure and sadness washed over her simultaneously. *Hope was right: he wants me back. And I don't know how to feel about it.*

She'd loved him. Nothing would ever change that, not even his betrayal. She'd fought so hard for them to be together, done everything she could to make him happy, which in turn had made her happy. But what now? What did she want? What made her happy now?

She needed to get to the office.

"Nice to see you again," she said simply as he opened the limo door for her, waited for her to get comfortable in the back seat and then slid in next to her, still holding the sunflower. She hadn't reached for it. She felt a lump in her throat at the sight of it, at the sight of him, her emotions so close to the surface, she had to use every ounce of strength to push them down, into a place from which she could summon them back up at some future time and examine them.

"I'm really glad you're here," said Rick. "You look lovely. No surprise there."

"Thanks for coming to pick me up," said Caroline. "Forrester Creations thinks of everything, even sending over my own personal Forrester escort."

He smiled. "This wasn't a company-sponsored idea. I just couldn't wait to see you."

"So Hope told me. How's Ridge doing?" she said, continuing to tamp down her conflicted feelings for him and steering the conversation away from their relationship. Too soon for that. If things went according to plan, she'd be in LA long enough for Rick to make his case and for her to respond accordingly. Meanwhile, she was focused on the task at hand: designing for the fashion show and helping the fundraiser go off without a hitch.

"I feel sorry for the guy," said Rick, laying the sunflower across his lap. "What he did, trying to get RJ and the other kid out of that house, was amazing, but if you think he didn't like me before, you should see how he treats me now."

"It isn't really about you, is it?" said Caroline. "He's the one who lost his eyesight."

He raised an eyebrow. "You're sticking up for him?"

"I asked how *he* was doing," she clarified. "I'll be working with him, so I have more than a passing interest."

"Yeah, well, good luck with that," said Rick. "I mean it, Caroline. We all need this collaboration between you to succeed. I'll do whatever I can to help."

"I appreciate that."

Rick spent the rest of the drive filling her in on the state of affairs at Forrester Creations. Ridge, he explained, kept to himself in his dimly lit office. Pam and Donna helped him navigate important files and documents requiring his attention or signature, but bright computer screens and tablets were off limits and he wore dark glasses at all times. Occasionally, he'd call a meeting, but mostly he worked on design sketches that never made it into production because they weren't developed enough to translate into concepts anybody could decipher. "He sees partial images, which is better than nothing," said Rick. "But his drawings look like Sudoku puzzles to me."

"Sounds grim," said Caroline. "I can't imagine what he's going through."

"The doctors say his vision will come back," said Rick. "Hell, it should have come back already. Maybe he and I should trade places. I'm stuck in the basement in Thorne's old office, with as much light as a cave."

Caroline nodded, trying to look sympathetic. And she did sympathize; Rick had been president of Forrester Creations until Ridge banished him. Not easy for any man, especially a man like Rick, who'd competed with Ridge for their father's approval for too many years to count.

As they pulled up to the entrance of Forrester Creations, Rick took Caroline's hand and looked her in the eyes. "Maya is not in the picture anymore," he said softly. "She won't be at the office, won't be at the guesthouse, isn't even in LA, so you don't need to worry about running into her, okay?"

"I wasn't worried about running into her," Caroline said, removing his hand from hers. "I was worried about running into you."

He smiled. "Wasn't that bad, was it?"

"No," she admitted. The surprise of his appearance at the hotel had given her a jolt, no question, but now she was relieved he'd come. Their drive to the office had broken the ice, gotten their first meeting over with, and she'd survived.

*

Ridge was pacing. Well, as much as you can pace when you have to be vigilant about not bumping into furniture or tripping over your own two feet. All he'd tried to do was walk over to the coffee table to eat a roast beef sandwich and he'd nearly broken a toe maneuvering around his desk, which was not exactly a high-wire act.

He stroked the coarse, straggly bush on his chin as he fumed. He'd grown the beard, along with his hair, which now dipped to the tops of his shoulder blades, because he'd given up trying to deal with a razor—the last time he'd made an attempt he'd ended up with more cuts and scrapes than a kid after a few rounds with a schoolyard bully—and he'd refused to allow that joker Monsieur Keith to come to the house and administer a shave and a haircut. Eric said he looked like a hippy and Brooke said he looked like a backwoodsman, but RJ said he looked like a "badass" and Ridge was fine with that. He was sure they all thought he was crazy, but his life had changed dramatically and he was struggling to adapt.

Who cares what everyone thinks? he reminded himself. *Sit the hell down and get to work.* He sank into his desk chair, and his sunglasses slipped down his nose as they often did when he so much as moved a muscle—another annoyance. He couldn't wait to get rid of the things, couldn't wait to turn on the lights, open the drapes, feel the sunshine on his face, all of it. He didn't regret having gone to Malibu and gotten RJ and Kyle out of that house, not for a second, and he'd do it all again in a heartbeat. It was just that the frustration of not being able to see normally kept building and building, and though he knew he had to be patient—all the doctors said so—he kept feeling *like* a patient, a victim, and it wasn't who he was; he was chairman and CEO of Forrester Creations with an important fundraiser coming up, and he needed his models to strut down the runway wearing an exclusive preview of his spring collection, couture dresses that the coiffed and bejeweled women in attendance at the fundraiser would pay anything to buy.

Of course, it would help if he weren't blocked creatively too.

A knock on the door interrupted his stream of extremely unproductive thinking. "What is it now?" he snapped and was immediately remorseful. It wasn't like him to be short with Pam or Donna. They were only trying to make things easier for him. Not fair to bite their heads off for it. "Come in, come in. Please."

"Ridge!" said the woman who practically sprinted into his office after closing the door behind her.

The voice didn't belong to either Pam or Donna. It was younger, perkier, more melodic. He squinted through his glasses, hoping to get a clearer idea of his visitor's identity before he had to suffer the indignity of asking. He couldn't quite make out her facial features—he could see only shadows with jagged lines and red spots running through them, thanks to his damaged retinas—but he couldn't miss the woman's trim body, her wavy, shoulder-length hair, the bounce in her step: Caroline. Of course. He'd forgotten she was supposed to show up.

"We meet again!" she said louder than was necessary, moving briskly toward his desk and waving her hands in the air at him like a sailor stranded in the middle of the ocean. "It's Caroline! Caroline Spencer. I came straight from my hotel after the jet landed!"

"My hearing's fine, so there's no need to shout," he growled, "or run like you have a train to catch; I'm not going anywhere. And my sight loss didn't cause memory loss. I think I can still remember your last name without any prompting, Caroline."

"Oh. Right. Sorry. Well, I'm here. Ready to roll up my sleeves and get busy. Should I pull up a chair next to yours or would you rather we sit over at the conference table? And before I forget, I'm very excited about working on the couture line. I mean, wow. Just *wow*. Designing with you for the fashion show? Awesome opportunity, plus it will be fun and productive. We'll meet the company's deadline, no worries, and I personally cannot wait to see the reaction at the fundraiser when everybody gets a look at what we've accomplished. It'll be a seriously spectacular event, don't you think?"

"My God." He sat back in his chair and shook his shaggy head. "Do you always talk so much?"

"Yes. No. I don't know." She paused. "I say we work at the conference table," she said, plunging back into the task at hand. "We'll have more room to spread out and compare sketches. Here, why don't you stand up and let me help you across the room."

Without waiting for an answer, she inched around his massive desk until she was close enough to take his elbow—but he jerked his arm away.

"Caroline," he said, standing up tall, adjusting his glasses. "I have limited sight in both eyes, so I can't see the bewildered expression on your face, but here's the deal. I am not an invalid. I do not need a nurse or a caretaker or a seeing-eye human. I can manage to get around my office on my own. Thank you."

He reached for his sketchpad, stepped tentatively around his desk and promptly crashed into the brass desk lamp, knocking it to the carpet with a thud.

Without missing a beat, she kneeled down to pick it up. "No harm done. Nothing broken."

"Leave it," Ridge instructed. "Not your job to clean up after me either."

"Right. Sorry."

"And please stop apologizing. There's been enough of that from the others."

Ridge could feel Caroline trailing behind him as he continued to the conference table.

"There," she said when they were each settled into chairs adjacent to each other. "Why don't I have a look at the sketches you've been playing with and you can explain your vision for each of them."

"I'm not *playing* with my sketches," he said. "I'm not five years old and they're not a bunch of Legos."

"Right. Sorry."

He slapped his sketchpad onto the table and turned toward her with a genuine scowl. "Did you not hear me at all? Are you lacking in auditory capability or are you just obtuse, as in dense, thick-headed, simple-minded?"

He watched her shadowy form rise from her chair, hands on her hips, and he assumed she was glaring down at him. "I'd really like to slap you right now, Ridge."

"Excuse me?"

"I said, I'd really like to slap you, but I'm not the slapping sort of person."

"Well, isn't that a relief."

"This whole ... tantrum thing of yours? I'm done with it already and I've only been here for like six minutes," she said. "I got up at dawn so I could fly across the country to help Forrester Creations and, by extension, *you*, with the fundraiser. Hope told me you'd agreed that I should pitch in, Ridge. You signed off on it. Why you did, I can't begin to understand, since all you've done since I walked in the door is berate me for my unsatisfactory vocabulary. I've never been in your situation—your sight loss, I mean—but I've spent many hours with men, women and children with cancer, some surviving it, some not." She paused to draw breath. Ridge shifted in his chair. "I don't sit in my crib sucking my thumb, is what I'm saying. So this will be the last time I apologize to you or watch my words around you or coddle you, and in turn I'd appreciate it if you'd kill the diva act. Do I make myself clear?"

Ridge sat silently, awed by Caroline's monologue. Then he raised his hands and began to slowly clap. "Quite a speech, Caroline Spencer, quite a speech." He stroked his beard and nodded approvingly at her. "I always did like your spirit, your fearlessness, and you've just reminded me why. I remember when I came back from Paris and told Rick I was taking his job away from him, and you called me out for it—vociferously. I still don't get what you saw in him, by the way. And I can't fathom how you could come from the same gene pool as your uncle Bill, one of the worst human beings I've ever met, but here you are. As soon as your little hissy fit's over, perhaps we could get to work."

"That's it? That's all you have to say?"

"Yes. We have a lot to do, so sit down. Please."

"Fine." She sat back down next to him and drew her chair closer.

She's not like anybody else, Ridge thought as he inhaled the sweet scent of her vanilla-infused fragrance, her lecture echoing in his mind. She'd been straight with him and she was right—he deserved her tongue-lashing. And she was very beautiful, whether he could make out the finer points of her face at this moment or not. If he could hold onto the last unadulterated image he had of her at Luc's in New York, of her wearing one of his designs, the black one with the sheer lace bodice, of her personality so light and bubbly, of her ease in social settings so classy and sophisticated yet with a touch of screwball, this arrangement of theirs just might not be so hard to take after all.

*

Caroline's task was to sort through Ridge's designs, figure out which were worth saving and make them happen. He had numbered each of the designs he'd sketched before the fire, and then there were the un-numbered sketches he'd struggled through after the fire.

"I envision this gown as the true harbinger of spring," Ridge said, pointing to a very rough sketch of a flowing, full-length dress cinched at the waist with a thin belt. There had been two dozen other drawings under discussion over their long, draining session, and while Caroline would have her work cut out for her to redraw, refine and reinterpret them for the seamstresses, they were trademark Forrester Creations designs even in their most rudimentary state. She and Ridge had only disagreed on a couple of his sketches, and their bickering had grown so heated he'd thought it had nearly sent her fleeing his office.

"It'll look like a toga," she'd said of one design, which featured an excess of silk to be draped around the model's back in pleated layers. "No, forget the toga. It'll look like a very expensive bed sheet."

"You're too young and too inexperienced to appreciate a concept like this," Ridge had sniffed. "No historical perspective."

"I'm not too young to know a woman likes to show off her curves, not bury them in fabric," she'd retorted.

"A woman who's comfortable with herself doesn't need to flaunt her curves."

"Please. Putting this dress on a woman would be like tenting her for termites."

"What did you just say to me?"

"The dress would look like it was designed to exterminate bugs, Ridge."

"You're embarrassing yourself, Caroline. You're really showing your unfamiliarity with couture."

"Oh, that's sweet," she said in her most saccharine voice meant to blunt his criticism. "But I think you meant to say, 'Thank you, Caroline, for giving me your honest assessment.'"

Ridge had backed down—temporarily. They'd moved on to the next drawing, a design that called for a sheer, gauzy, beaded silk with long sleeves and a high neck accentuated with a crystal brooch. Caroline had dubbed it matronly. Ridge had countered that it was vintage inspired. Caroline had come back with: "Inspired by Grandma's closet." He'd told her she probably took her fashion cues from Miley Cyrus. She'd answered that she was surprised he knew who Miley Cyrus was, given his advancing years. At one point, their voices must have been raised loud and long enough that Pam knocked on the door and asked if everything was all right. They'd both yelled, "Fine!" and went back at it.

If this is what day one is like, we'll murder each other by the time the fashion show rolls around, he'd thought.

Thank goodness the subsequent designs created no such tension, and their exchanges were far less contentious, even complimentary.

"Yes, in this one, maybe the woman is taking a trip to the tropics to kick off the spring season," said Ridge of the belted design, "which is why I'm seeing lily pads or a jungle print or even a floral pattern straight out of an Impressionist painting."

Caroline nodded. "Exactly—the perfect contrast to the designs that were more monochromatic. I loved their pale palette of teals, peach and white, so airy and uncomplicated. But with this one and its splashes of color, we're talking about the showstopper. It could be that good, Ridge—arresting visually but with a sense of grace, elegance and ease. I like it for the finale. A lot."

"Well, what do you know? I guess I should be doing cartwheels or something," Ridge said wryly, sitting back in his chair. "Caroline Spencer, the arbiter of fashion, has given it her blessing." He was sarcastic, but secretly he was pleased. No one else at the company had understood what he'd done, let alone liked it. She was a worthy adversary who didn't "yes" him to death and he appreciated that. He appreciated her *and* her brutal candor. He liked being around her, liked the way she pushed him to be better. Even when she poked and prodded and mocked him, he'd felt more alive than he had since the fire, his emotions veering from wanting to strangle her to wanting to …

Wanting to what? Ridge asked himself. Was he so starved for a woman's affection since burrowing into his lonely cave that he was ready to fall for anyone in high heels and a skirt? No. That wasn't it. He'd always thought she was special—a knockout but whip-smart too. He'd been reminded of that when they'd seen each other at Luc's opening in New York. He'd had the fleeting impulse to kiss her that night, when he'd fed her that amuse-bouche, and it took him completely by surprise, since she was not only too young for him but most likely still carrying a torch for Rick.

She's not interested in damaged goods like you, Forrester. Don't even go there, he told himself. *Keep it strictly professional. Your collaboration just started and there are sure to be bumps in the road, but there was progress today, so enjoy that and forget the rest.*

As he was shuffling through the designs, his glasses slipped down the bridge of his nose again and in an effort to push them back in place he knocked them off, onto the floor. He lowered himself off the chair and began to feel around the carpet for them.

"Let me," said Caroline, bending down to scoop them up. She was about to position the glasses back on his face when he snatched them away from her and adjusted them himself. He felt exposed without the sunglasses, vulnerable, and he didn't like the feeling at all.

"I told you, it's not your job to pick up after me," he said brusquely.

"Right. Sorry."

There was another knock on the door and Ridge told Pam they were done with the meeting. Into the office walked Thomas. Caroline jumped up to greet him, while Ridge walked slowly to his desk.

"Hey, Caroline. Welcome back," said Thomas with a big, toothy grin, extending his hand for her to shake.

She pulled him into a hug instead. "Why so formal? It's just me, Thomas."

"I'm really happy you're here. We all are," he said, then glanced over at his father. "Work productive this afternoon, Dad?"

"Ask her," Ridge growled, back in curmudgeon mode. "She seems to think she's running this show."

Caroline laughed. "Yes, Thomas. It was productive. Your dad's still got it."

"So do you. You look great."

"And you look every bit the president of Forrester Creations in that gray suit. One of your designs?"

He nodded shyly. "I try to be a good ad for the product."

"You're succeeding."

"Would you two mind taking this chummy conversation outside so I can hear myself think?"

Thomas smiled, offering Caroline his elbow. "I was just about to ask if you have dinner plans tonight or are you too jet-lagged?"

"Actually, I'm having dinner with my uncle Bill," Caroline said. "We're going to—"

"Was I talking to myself?" Ridge barked. "Out."

Chapter Five

"So, how's the Chosen One these days?" Bill Spencer smirked as only he could smirk. It was almost a snarl, his lips curling underneath the mustache of his neatly trimmed goatee. He hated Ridge Forrester and made no secret of it.

"He's hurting," Caroline said as she sipped wine at his Malibu beach house before dinner. "I think the bravado is all a front to mask how helpless and alone he feels since the fire."

"Give me a break with the violins, would you please?" He was dressed in all black, as usual, his shirt open to reveal his silver sword necklace, the one that seemed to embody his warrior, often cutthroat, ethic. "Don't get me wrong. I wouldn't want to be in his shoes with the eye thing—definitely not fun—but the guy's been full of bravado since he came out of the womb, and the joke of it is, he doesn't have a clue what he wants or what to do with it once he gets it. He jerked Brooke around for years and she was the best thing that ever happened to him."

"To you too?" Caroline asked with a knowing smile. She guessed her uncle still loved Brooke Logan even if they did have a tangled history, but he managed to keep himself very busy with a procession of other women and he was never short of bed partners.

"Yeah, yeah." He took a healthy swig of his scotch. "Which is why you should give Rick another shot."

Caroline set down her wineglass, her eyebrow arched. "What? Why would you want me to? He betrayed me, Uncle Bill."

"He made a mistake, no argument from me there. But I respect a man who makes a mistake and says he's sorry. He came to me weeks ago and asked me to plead his case with you—you'll notice I stayed out of it—and I believe he's sincere. And besides, he's Brooke's son. So do me a favor and give the kid another chance, huh?"

"Just like that? I'm supposed to forgive him? Trust him? Feel about him the way I used to?"

"Why not?" he scoffed. "You two made a good team, remember? And I need a Spencer looking out for my interests at Forrester Creations. I have a stake in that company, let's not forget, and I can't leave it to their current CEO to manage the place, not when he's doing his best Stevie Wonder routine."

"Uncle Bill!" Bill Spencer was nothing if not tell it like it is, and his comments could be politically incorrect and crude and were frequently both. "I'm here to do a job, to help Ridge finish designing for their fashion show fundraiser, so be nice."

He reached out to pat her on the head. "I'll be nice." He smiled in that naughty way of his. He could be tender when the moment called for it and family did mean a lot to him, but if you were unlucky enough to get on his bad side, watch out. "Here's how nice I'll be. I'm getting up out of this comfortable chair to throw a couple of prime tenderloins on the grill, so be a good niece and set the table."

*

Caroline slept deeply, so tired from the traveling and the intense first day of work that she decided to languish in bed the next morning and have her breakfast delivered. She was browsing her favorite fashion sites on her tablet when her room service tray arrived with a surprise: a single sunflower along with a note. She recognized the scrawl on the outside of the ivory envelope and felt her pulse quicken. She slid her knife under the seal and opened it.

Dear Caroline,

I've never been much of a writer—Ridge seems to be the Forrester poet laureate—so I hope you'll forgive me if some of this sounds like the diary entry of a teenager. Well, I hope you'll forgive me for a lot of things, but I'll get to them later in this letter, which I'm delivering not in a text or an email but the old-fashioned way, the more romantic, timeless way (in my opinion).

I've done a lot of soul-searching over the many months since you left LA and had a lot of those "Who are you, Rick Forrester, and what do you want to be when you grow up?" conversations with myself. Sad, isn't it? I should have done all this when I was sixteen or even twenty. But some people take longer to figure things out, and I guess I'm one of them.

I grew up with chaos, as you know. My parents split up and my sister Bridget and I were never exactly sure what happened until we were older. But our parents loved us, each in their own way, and I should have focused on that instead of on what was missing, how I felt abandoned, how I felt like the forgotten son. I'm not telling you this so you'll feel sorry for me. I was a lucky, privileged kid. I had every material advantage—the best schools, the fastest cars, the houses with more square feet than we needed, the easy access to the family business.

But I was always trying to find my place in the scheme of things, create some stability for myself. Instead, I kept screwing up, attaching myself to the wrong people—the wrong women—and I ended up creating the same kind of chaos I grew up with because it was familiar.

You're probably sitting there laughing as you read this and wondering if some shrink put words in my mouth. For better or worse, I came to these conclusions all by myself.

What I'm saying is I kept repeating the pattern of being the family screw-up, over and over—until I met you. You were the first thing in my life that made sense. You were the opposite of a screw-up, Caroline. You knew what you wanted out of life and you went for it. You even went for me. And you stuck with me no matter how badly I treated you. How did you do that? What gave you the strength to do that? And how the hell could I have let you slip away?

I was still in that little boy's head, that's how—the little boy who was always recreating the chaos he grew up with. Crazy, right?

Here's what I know now, in the dawn hours as I write this: I'm done with chaos, done with being the screw-up. I want another chance with you, to prove that I'm more together, more aware of my shortcomings and how to fix them. Do I deserve another chance? Only you can decide that, but I hope you'll at least take this time while you're in LA to let me convince you.

We could start tonight, if you're willing. Have dinner with me, Caroline. Hear me out. Or don't hear me out, just share a meal with me, talk about the weather, it doesn't matter. It'll be a fresh start and I'll grab it with both hands.

All my love,

Rick

Caroline placed the letter on the bed beside her, sank back against her thick pile of feather pillows and let her mind replay Rick's words. He had never taken the time to write her a letter before. He was more of a doer than a thinker, more prone to taking action than mulling things over. She'd hardly qualify him as introspective and self-exploring—that was Ridge to a T—but maybe the divorce had really shaken him, made him examine where he'd been going wrong.

And maybe it was only fair to let him try to make things right. One dinner, not a lifetime commitment, was all he was asking for. Just one dinner.

Oh, why not, she thought, sitting up in bed now, pulling her breakfast tray closer. *What harm could it do?*

*

"Here I am," said Caroline as she marched into Ridge's office.

"Did we sleep in?" Ridge said from behind his desk. "I can't see the time on my watch, obviously," he said, giving his well-worn, brown leather-strapped Cartier a look anyway, "but I'm fairly sure it's not 'first thing in the morning,' as we'd agreed."

"You're right," she said, placing her tote bag on his desk and then pulling over one of the visitor's chairs and settling into it. "But I spent hours in my hotel going over my notes from yesterday and I think I've come up with a good working agenda to give you and the production staff."

"You're at a hotel?"

"Yes. Hope put me up at the Beverly Wilshire, which is lovely. Thank you."

"I thought you'd be staying at the dreaded Bill Spencer's house," said Ridge.

"I saw Uncle Bill last night," said Caroline. "He sends his best wishes."

"I'll bet. What about the guesthouse with Rick? You've seen him since you arrived, yes?" He really couldn't imagine what she'd been thinking, marrying that preening pretty boy, and he hoped her accepting the assignment at Forrester Creations wasn't motivated by her desire to get back together with him. She could do so much better. If things were different, if he wasn't as old as her uncle, if he wasn't so detached from even the idea of a relationship, if he wasn't impaired, unfit to romance any woman let alone shave his own face, he would act on his attraction to her without a second thought. He'd felt it in New York at Luc's opening. There'd been a connection between them, a chemistry. But what was he supposed to do about it now? Unless his sight returned, he was better off alone, better not to be a burden to anyone. Still, he wished he could emerge from behind the sunglasses to see her clearly, her playful eyes, lush lips and porcelain skin, see how snugly her clothes clung to every curve of her body, see how her legs seemed to go on forever ...

"So," she said, letting his queries about her ex-husband hang in the air, "I'll run my ideas by you and you can tell me yes or no." She fished her tablet out of the tote bag and clicked on her meeting agenda. "Here's my proposed order for the designs. We launch the fashion show with design number four, the peach gown with the halter top. Then we bring out design number six ..." She went through her entire list, careful not to omit the pair of designs they'd squabbled over—the termite tent and the dowdy dud—but rather to describe how she would simplify the former and enliven the latter. And then she suggested accessories for each dress—jewelry, shoes, hairstyles and makeup—and the right model to wear each one. She'd imagined every aspect of the fashion show right down to the music, and he could hear in her voice how much she had loved doing it.

Her presentation lasted into the afternoon. When she finished, she exhaled. He realized she was proud of the hard work she'd put in so soon after arriving in LA. She'd hit the ground running, acutely aware that there was a ticking clock with the fundraiser looming. Of course Ridge hadn't uttered a single word while she'd laid out her elaborate plans, not wanting to interrupt her. He hadn't even groaned or shaken his head in disapproval. She looked at him now expectantly.

"Nothing?" she asked.

"You've rendered me speechless," he said wryly in an effort to cover what was really going on inside his head. "Your talent and efficiency almost make me want to cry, Caroline." He pretended to wipe a tear from beneath his glasses.

"Oh, cut it out, Ridge. You're wasting valuable time with that nonsense. We've got a show to put on."

"You're right again." He gave her a little salute. "Blame it on this ridiculous—" He pointed to his eyes. "It's messed with my manners and I'm sorry. I was very impressed by your descriptions, and there's not a thing in any of them that I would change."

It was the truth: Ridge was amazed by the scope of her presentation and by how quickly and thoroughly she'd tackled every design. But he'd been distracted while she was talking, something that happened to him all too frequently since the fire. He'd find himself concentrating on business and then descend into a flashback of that terrible day in Malibu canyon, the thick plumes of smoke making the air nearly impossible to breathe, the threatening embers licking at the roof, the urgency of getting the boys out of the house and into the car, the sudden collapse of the roof and the thunderous, apocalyptic blast of the house igniting, the excruciating pain as he stared into that orange fireball. His eyes still burned with the memory. The doctors said the sensation would pass as the retinal cells regenerated, but the waiting seemed eternal. He'd had enough of it and wanted his life back.

"Ridge?" said Caroline. "Are you okay?"

"Fine," he said, snapping back to the matter at hand. "I would have fought for the 'termite tent' to stay in your line-up of the designs, but I thought about it last night and you did have a point. So I'm approving the changes. Good work, Caroline. No, make that great work."

Caroline couldn't contain herself. She raised her arms in the air and let out a "Woo hoo," which made Ridge laugh.

"Don't get too comfortable and think the rest of it will be as easy," he cautioned. "Fashion shows for the couture line are a tricky business."

"Believe me, none of what you heard today was easy," she said with a laugh of her own. "I second-guessed myself a hundred times before coming to you today."

"Somehow I doubt that." He stared at her from behind the dark glasses. "Would you mind putting your presentation into a memo to staff and Pam or Donna will circulate it so the other departments can get started?"

"I've already done that, since time is such a factor. Given the memo to Donna, I mean. She won't circulate it until she has your okay."

He smiled. "Sure of yourself, weren't you?"

"No, just hopeful."

She was special all right, on top of every detail, large or small. How did Forrester Creations ever manage without her? How did *he* ever manage without her? He was drawn to her, drawn to the light and energy she radiated whenever she bounced into a room, drawn to the sound of her melodic voice, drawn to the scent of her perfume, drawn to the way she made him laugh when nobody or nothing else could. She flat-out fascinated him and he suddenly wanted to know her better. He'd been in Paris during most of her first go-around at Forrester Creations and had missed her star turn, designing for Hope for the Future. He'd heard from Thomas how she'd bailed out Rick when the line had taken a dive in sales, how she was the driving force behind its surge in popularity. He'd missed Rick's courtship of her too, along with their Thanksgiving wedding at his parents' house, thankfully. All he knew about her, other than her Spencer background, was that

Brooke had lured her to LA to work with Rick and pry him away from yet another failing relationship—and that it had worked out for all concerned until Rick had failed with Caroline too. But who was she really? What made her tick? Who was this woman to whom he had entrusted his designs and his fundraiser for his mother and who, whether he liked it or not, was beginning to inch her way into his heart?

Ridge placed his hands behind his head and leaned back in his chair. "So, since we've handled our business today and I have nothing else that's pressing at the moment, tell me about you, Caroline."

"About me?" she asked.

"Tell me about yourself, your personal goals, your interests. Are there places in the world where you'd like to travel? Do you dream of having kids? Do you have a favorite movie? A favorite book? A favorite food—although I remember that it's not gruyere gougères."

"Hey, I did like those little hors d'oeuvres," she said. "I just didn't recite poetry about them the way you did."

"I'll have you getting poetic about food yet, you wait. But back to you, tell me whatever you want, Caroline Spencer. What was it like growing up in New York, which way do you lean politically, what interests you outside of fashion?" he said.

"There must be something you enjoy outside of designing," Ridge prodded when he noticed she was uncharacteristically quiet.

"Not so much," she admitted with a sheepish laugh. "I mean there's my foundation for cancer research. Otherwise, I'm not that well read and my movie-going experiences tend toward whatever's playing at the multiplexes and I don't pay a lot of attention to politics. As for traveling, I'm ashamed to say I haven't traveled a lot except with my mother for occasional Spencer Publications business. I've never been to Paris, if you can believe it. I've been single-minded about designing and moving up in the industry, I guess."

"Never been to Paris? Oh, Caroline." He sighed. "What you've been missing. Life is short, you know." He paused. "Okay, I'm giving you an assignment. It's multifaceted and it has nothing to do with the fashion show. I want you to take yourself to one of the art-house cinemas in town and watch a foreign film—with subtitles. I want you to read something other than *Vogue*: a novel you think might move you or a biography of someone you admire. I want you to get tickets for a sporting event—Lakers, Clippers, Dodgers, Kings; doesn't matter. We aren't necessarily known as a sports town here in LA and you don't strike me as the athletic type, but we've got some very good teams and you should go to a game or two because the crowds get rowdy and fun and there's nothing like it when your team wins. I want you to eat at LA's best restaurants—not the standard-issue, white-tablecloth, overpriced, expense-account establishments, but the ethnic places, the food trucks, the joints where the chefs are taking risks—and savor the food as if it was your last meal, not just wolf it down because you're hungry. And when all this fundraiser stuff is over and you have the time, I want you to hightail it out of LA and New York—book yourself on a trans-Atlantic flight and go to Paris, and then go to London and Rome and Barcelona and Sydney and anyplace else that arouses your curiosity. But get out of the bubble, Caroline, and do it while you still can."

"Is that why you went to Paris, Ridge? To get out of the bubble? I thought you went there to run Forrester International."

"I did, but also to experience the city and the people," said Ridge. "I'd been to Paris many times, but I'd never seized the opportunity to enjoy living there, to explore new neighborhoods, go to museums, immerse myself in the French culture. Getting out of the bubble is how we learn about the world, learn about ourselves too." He leaned forward in his chair and shrugged. "Forgive me. I sound like some washed-up old college professor giving a tedious lecture."

Caroline shook her head. "I liked what you said. I just wish you didn't think I was so one-dimensional."

"No, not one-dimensional, Caroline Spencer," he said softly, kindly, almost affectionately, a tone he wasn't used to using. "Definitely not that."

✻

Her mind reeling from their conversation, Caroline hurried to her scheduled meeting with Hope, who rushed to the door to greet her, crushing her in a hug. Rick's younger sister was still so lovely—a blue-eyed princess, a honey-blond prom queen, her wholesome youth having given way to a strong, sexy, independent young woman whose message reached legions of young women around the world with her clothing line.

"So? How did Ridge like everything?" Hope asked with breathless anticipation. "I've been checking my watch every five minutes, wondering what was going on down the hall. I almost texted you."

"Sorry, we ran late," said Caroline. Was her face flushed? It felt that way, almost as if she and Ridge had shared an intimate experience, not merely a professional one. "He liked my presentation a lot, Hope. I think it's all going to work out."

"Yes!" Hope squealed. "I knew it! If anyone could get through to Ridge it would be you, Caroline. You're awesome, and I'm so grateful. We all are." She hugged her again. "What's the next step?"

"You'll be getting the line-up for the fashion show today, and hopefully production and marketing will work their magic. I can't wait to see it all take shape."

Hope giggled. "That's all great, but I meant what's the next step for you?" Her eyes twinkled. "Rick said there might be a romantic dinner-for-two tonight?"

Caroline smiled, appreciative of Hope's eagerness to help her reconcile with Rick and of her good intentions, but careful not to convey any false promises. "I'll be having dinner with Rick tonight, yes. But we're divorced, Hope. There was a reason we split up and I hadn't seen him in six months until yesterday. The whole idea of us getting back together is totally new for me and I don't even know how I feel about it. So it's much too soon for some romantic candlelight thing. It would be inappropriate at best."

Chapter Six

"A quiet table by the fireplace, sir, as you requested," said the tuxedoed maître d' as he bowed with the deference of someone who'd already been given a healthy tip. He pulled out Caroline's lushly upholstered high-back chair, and made sure she was comfortable before placing a white linen napkin across her lap and unfolding a small rattan stand on which he deposited her purse. He turned to place Rick's napkin across his lap, then said, "I'll send your server over right away."

"Right away" apparently meant right that very second, because a young man wearing a crisp white shirt with a black tie and black pants appeared with leather-bound menus weighing as much as old telephone books.

Next came a veritable cavalcade of other, equally fawning, black and white clad servers.

The first delivered a bread tray offering six options, from a warm potato roll to a cone-shaped baguette, accompanied by small ramekins of truffle butter, almond butter and olive butter. He was followed by the "water sommelier," who announced selections of water, both still and sparkling, from ten different countries, including California's own limited edition "vintage water." He made way for the "master sommelier," who, before turning over the wine list to Rick, recited his credentials and imparted the intended note of gravitas to the occasion. Eventually, the "server-in-chief," as he referred to himself, showed up to report the chef's recommendations of the day and asked, "Is this a special occasion for the two of you? A birthday or anniversary, perhaps?"

Caroline couldn't help thinking of Ridge throughout the evening, kept hearing his words reverberate in her mind. The restaurant Rick had chosen for their first dinner together since the divorce was exactly the kind of place Ridge had told her to avoid in order to get out of the bubble, a "standard-issue, white-tablecloth, overpriced, expense-account establishment." It was also pretentious and silly—the sort of fussy, stereotypical restaurant where men routinely took their dates to propose or celebrate Valentine's Day. All of which would have been perfectly fine with Caroline if she and Rick were, indeed, celebrating something but, as she told Hope, it was much too soon for that.

She did appreciate being seated next to the fireplace, though. Dense fog—the marine layer, they called it in California—had blanketed LA by sunset and the air had turned chilly and damp. She'd paid little attention to the weather forecast and regretted it. She hadn't dressed appropriately, given her sleeveless cowl neck top and short skirt, not bothering with a sweater or jacket. Despite her East Coast roots, she felt the cold more keenly in California, and was shivering until the fireplace began to warm her.

Rick looked as handsome as ever in his elegant, custom-made suit, his hair slicked back off his finely chiseled face, his scent reminding her of their languid nights in bed when they made love again and again until they finally fell asleep in each other's arms. All was right with the world then. Caroline really believed that. She'd viewed Rick Forrester as if he were a reward—the prize she'd won in the hard-fought competition with Maya. She'd thought the contest was over, and they would thrive as Mr and Mrs Eric Forrester, Jr, a fashion industry power couple whose comings and goings would be chronicled in glossy international magazines, Spencer Publications' own *Eye on Fashion* included. It was a fairy tale, she realized now, as she watched him drain his wine goblet. *They* were a fairy tale, and fairy tales were for children.

"This is nice," he said during one of the five or six courses, Caroline couldn't keep track of them.

"Being here with you is like old times. I haven't been this happy in—well, since you left."

He took her hand, brought it up to his lips and kissed it. The dinner hadn't started out with compliments and kisses. Rick had ordered wine for them and asked her if she was warm enough and quizzed her about her meeting with Ridge. But it was obvious to Caroline from the outset that he had more on his mind than small talk. She could tell by the way he worked his jaw and flexed his fingers that there was pent-up nervous energy he needed to exorcize, that he was dying to talk about a possible reconciliation, about whether they could begin again, about whether she would forgive him and take him back.

When he finally did delve into their relationship, he expanded on what he'd written in the letter, about his chaotic adolescence and his pattern of screwing up. It was an effort to explain his behavior, explain about Maya, explain how his self-esteem was so low after Ridge kicked him out of the president's office that he grabbed for the nearest fix, the quickest numbing agent, and Maya was it.

"Why didn't you come to me instead of her?" Caroline asked, the question she'd considered many times in the six months since the divorce. "We were supposed to be a team and teammates stick together, for better or worse."

"I know that now," he said, holding her gaze. "I guess I was ashamed to come to you. You had such high expectations for me, Caroline. Maybe I didn't want to let you down."

"So you let me down in the worst possible way," she mused. She did have high expectations for him, just as she'd had for them as a couple, but she'd been his best sounding board and never judged him, always tried to cheer him up when things didn't go in his favor. Caroline suddenly had a thought: Rick never asked her about herself, not like Ridge had earlier, never like that. In fact, the letter he'd written focused on *his* needs, *his* shortcomings and *his* childhood hurts, just like this conversation. And it had ended with an invitation to dinner so he could "pour *his* heart out." At no point in the letter did he say, "I want to hear about *you*, about *your* life."

"If Ridge hadn't come back from Paris, maybe none of this would have happened," Rick muttered now. "It all went downhill from there."

"You're seriously blaming Ridge for your affair with Maya?" Caroline said hotly. "He didn't force you to reach out to her, to sleep with her, to blow up our marriage." She was appalled, and the fact that she was appalled surprised her. Before she came back to LA, she'd resented Ridge almost as much as Rick did. She'd bought the argument about how Rick's demotion had been so unfair, so egregious, that it had caused him to act irrationally, and she, too, had demonized Ridge. But while Ridge did have a low opinion of Rick and his promotion of his son Thomas was questionable, he certainly wasn't responsible for the breakup. She could see that clearly now.

And she could see how Ridge seemed to value her in a manner that Rick no longer did, if ever. Although his eyesight was compromised, Ridge had this uncanny knack for looking right through her, into her heart and soul. They'd only worked together for a mere two days, but they'd been intense, and she'd felt useful again, appreciated. He stimulated her not just to create better, bolder designs, but to question her goals in life, venture out of her comfort zone and grow, explore the world and her own thoughts and feelings, stop rushing around getting things done and checking items off a to-do list and instead get out there and see, smell, touch, use all her senses. He'd said as much as far back as the party at Luc's but she hadn't really heard him, hadn't let his words register. She'd always been in the bubble, ever since she was a little girl drawing dresses instead of playing a musical instrument or sticking her nose in a book. She'd had stirrings of wanting to broaden her interests and tastes but had never quite known how. Now she realized Ridge was so much more interesting than she'd ever given him credit for, and she was excited about spending more time with him. She had a sneaking suspicion he didn't mind having her around either. It dawned on her that his opinion mattered to her—not just his opinion of her designs but what was inside her. She knew she looked good on the outside; she'd had enough men fall all over her to understand the affect her appearance had on them and she spent enough on clothes and beauty products to enhance what nature had given her. But did any of these men take her seriously as a person with more going on in her head than the quest for the perfect little black dress? Did she even take herself seriously that way?

"Look, I don't like Ridge," said Rick. "No secret there. Half the time I walk around wanting to punch the guy in the face. The other half just wants him to fly back to Paris and stay there. I hate to think of you having to be cooped up in that office with him, Caroline. Must be torture."

"Not at all, actually," she said after a pause, a flush spreading across her cheeks.

Rick cocked his head at her. "What's this? You changing teams on me?"

When Caroline hesitated for just an instant, Rick's brows furrowed. "I can deal with you needing more time to trust me, to let me show you how much you mean to me and how badly I want us back together, but I couldn't handle it if you ever chose him over me. It would start a war, Caroline."

A war? Caroline knew Rick could be hotheaded, but his choice of words set off alarm bells. He and Ridge had done verbal battle too many times to count over the years, starting long before she'd ever met either of them, and a couple of those battles had resulted in hand-to-hand combat. The last thing Forrester Creations needed during the countdown to the fundraiser was any sort of family conflict, especially over her.

Besides, it was all so ridiculous. Caroline's interest in Ridge was purely professional and vice versa. She needed to diffuse the sudden tension at the table and she did so by laughing. "Nobody's doing any choosing," she assured Rick, reaching out to stroke his cheek, the first time she'd initiated any physical contact between them. "We really shouldn't be focusing on Ridge when this night is about us, isn't it?"

His face relaxed into a smile. "Now that's what I'm talking about," he said. "*Us.* I like the sound of that."

He leaned over to kiss her and she gently placed her hand on his chest.

"Too soon, Rick," she said. "I'm not saying it'll never happen. I'm not putting a timetable on it. I'm just asking if we could take baby steps. I'm still getting used to the idea of being back here, you know?"

He nodded. "Of course. I don't want to rush you. I just want you to know where I stand ... whenever you're ready."

*

The fog was so thick as they drove back to Beverly Hills from Santa Monica that they could barely see the hood of the Porsche, much less the other cars in front of them. It was treacherous, and Caroline wished they could pull over and wait out the fog, but that wasn't how it worked with marine layers; they often hung around for days. So Rick continued to drive, slowly, carefully. "I have to protect my precious cargo," he said, patting her knee.

They were going no more than forty miles an hour on the freeway when Rick spotted a car parked on the shoulder, a woman standing outside it, waving frantically for help.

"We should stop," he said, slowing down so he could park behind the car.

"Yes, good idea." Caroline smiled knowingly at Rick as he fished his flashlight out of the glove compartment. She did love that about him, how he enjoyed being the white knight to damsels in distress, except, of course, when the damsel was Maya. He had a kind heart. She'd seen it many times. It only disappeared when he thought his manhood was threatened—by Ridge.

The woman's Honda Accord had been rear-ended by another car whose driver had kept going—a combination fender-bender and hit-and-run—and she had cuts and bruises as well as a sore neck and back. She'd called 911 for assistance but the California Highway Patrol must have had a busy night, because it had been over two hours and they still hadn't come.

Rick offered to call a friend who volunteered as an EMT, and within thirty minutes the medics arrived to examine the woman and take her to the nearest hospital. She was extremely grateful to Rick, and Caroline was proud of his willingness to lend a hand without having to be asked.

She was also freezing. Not wanting to seem insensitive, she'd stood outside in the damp night air, waiting for help to arrive, instead of taking shelter in the Porsche. Rick wrapped his jacket over her shoulders and it did add a layer between her and the dampness, but her teeth were still chattering by the time they got back on the freeway.

"Do you feel feverish?" asked Rick as he bumped up the heat in the car. "I don't want you catching pneumonia on my watch."

"I'll be fine," she said. "I can't afford to be sick, not with the fashion show coming up."

"Then let me take care of you," he said. "Just for tonight. No strings. I promise."

"Oh, Rick. That's sweet, but I'll be okay. Really."

"No arguments. We'll go straight to your hotel and I'll order you a pot of hot tea, put you in bed, pile on the blankets and be there to check on you all night."

"All night? I don't think that's a good—"

"You're in a suite, Caroline," he reminded her. "There's a sleeper sofa in the living room. I'll tuck you in, say goodnight and close your door. I'll be right nearby if you need me but out of your way if you don't. Let me do this for you. I have so much to make up for."

She tried to protest again that she'd be fine on her own, but he wouldn't hear of it. He wanted to protect her, to show her he was the sort of man she could count on, nothing more.

"It's a beginning," he reminded her. "A baby step, just like you said."

Back at the Beverly Wilshire, Rick did exactly as he'd promised, the perfect gentleman. He ordered the tea while she changed into her nightgown, helped her into the king-size bed, asked housekeeping for an extra comforter and laid it gently on top of her to make sure she was warm enough and then he kissed her on the forehead, turned off the lights and headed for the adjacent living room.

"Sleep well, Caroline," he whispered.

"You too," she said. "And thanks, Rick."

He smiled and tiptoed out.

Chapter Seven

In the shower the next morning, Caroline let the hot water rain down on her body, cleansing her, warming her and rinsing away any residual chill from the night before. As she soaked in the gentle spray, she thought she heard a muffled male voice, from somewhere in her hotel suite. And then she laughed at herself, so lost in the lavender scent of the hotel's bath gel that she'd forgotten Rick was in the next room. Maybe he was watching the news on TV? Maybe he was checking in with the office? She thought back to the mornings they'd shared as a married couple in the Forrester guesthouse—a pleasant memory until the image of finding him with Maya brought her back to reality.

Rick had spent the night on the sofa, didn't intrude on her, didn't make any moves or demands, was respectful of the space she'd asked for while she considered his apology and decided whether or not they might have another chance. She had no idea how she felt about him now, but she did enjoy having his company, for old times' sake if nothing else. It had been months since a man had spent the night with her, and while her sleepover with Rick had been strictly platonic, it reminded her that she hadn't joined a convent and that she wanted and needed male companionship in her life.

She finished her shower and wrapped herself in the hotel's fluffy white robe, sweeping up and enfolding her wet hair in a large towel, before stepping out to join Rick.

"Don't you look ravishing?" he said with a grin. "Like a Greek goddess."

She laughed. "Thank you. I do feel a lot better."

"Good. Your eggs and coffee await." He eyed their breakfast and waved her over to sit beside him. "Dig in."

"Yum," she said after a healthy bite of a buttery croissant. "So delicious and so fattening."

"Ha. Like you need to worry about your figure. Indulge. You're on vacation."

"I most certainly am not," she said, continuing to devour the flaky pastry. "I should be dressed and out the door instead of sitting here stuffing my face. Ridge wants us to walk production through every design for the fashion show."

"Ridge," he muttered as he sipped his coffee. "Don't ruin both our appetites."

Caroline nodded, careful not to say any more about her boss—Rick's boss too, for that matter—so as not to further enflame their hostility toward each other.

But Rick wasn't finished venting. "The way he issues his *urgent* executive commands makes me sick."

"No, it was nothing like that," she said quietly. "We need to get the designs into production as soon as possible, that's all."

Rick's expression turned dark. "I should be not only involved in this fundraiser but running it," he said, not bothering to disguise his bitterness. "Instead, my job for the day will be pedaling my mother's lingerie line to a buyer in the North Pole or someplace equally irrelevant to the company's success."

Caroline stopped eating as he continued to complain about his reduced status at Forrester Creations. She'd heard it all before, and she was weary of it. "Rick, I'm sure if you keep working hard and prove yourself, things will get better and you'll move back upstairs. Ridge even said so."

"Is that what he told you?" He laughed scornfully. "Look, Caroline, you should be working with me on the designs for the fashion show, not Ridge. You were my designer before you left the company, my collaborator on Hope for the Future. We were a package deal and I shouldn't have been cut out of it."

"You weren't cut out of anything," said Caroline, trying not to let irritation creep into her voice. "Ridge's eyes were damaged in that fire and Hope said he needed my help. End of story."

Caroline didn't like that Rick felt proprietary and possessive of her after one dinner together nor that he wasn't showing the least bit of compassion for Ridge's condition. They were divorced, no longer a couple, just two people moving slowly toward a friendship again—a friendship that may or may not progress into something deeper. Yes, it was nice of him to spend the night, to care for her, fuss over her, but his latest tirade about Ridge was a turn-off.

"Hey," said Rick, gazing across the table at her. "Are we okay or did I just create a problem? I can't help it if I don't like you having to spend so much time with King Ridge."

Keep it light, she told herself. *Keep it positive. Don't say anything that will cause turmoil for Forrester Creations, not with so much riding on the success of the fundraiser. Keep the peace between him and Ridge whatever you have to do.*

"No problem," she said, finishing off the last remnants of the croissant and getting up from the table. "But I really should get moving. So should you. You need to go home and change clothes."

"The guesthouse is just around the corner, remember?" he said, stepping closer. He cupped her chin in his hand and tilted it up to meet his eyes. "I love seeing you in the morning, Caroline.

You're as beautiful in that bathrobe fresh out of the shower as you are dressed up in a Forrester Creations original."

"I must look a mess, but I'm grateful for the compliment. Thanks again for taking such good care of me, Rick. It was above and beyond the call of duty."

"It's not a duty to take care of you," he said earnestly. "I just hope you'll let me do it on a full-time basis like I used to—and soon." He looked like he was about to kiss her, then restrained himself. "And hey, I was a good boy all night, right? I didn't even try to sneak into your bedroom and crawl under all those blankets with you. You *can* trust me again."

He smiled hopefully. She knew he was serious about wanting her to trust him—and not just about spending the night in her hotel suite. He wanted her to know that there would be no more screw-ups, no more lies, no more sneaking around behind her back, only honesty.

"I'm very proud of you for staying on that sofa all night and showing such fortitude," she teased. "See you later at the office."

*

Ridge's back was to the door, his desk chair facing toward the wall, and he was listening to Bach, when he heard Caroline arrive for their meeting.

"Good morning, Ridge," she said, planting herself in the chair opposite his desk. "Perfect timing! You can educate me about this music you're listening to. I'm clueless, I admit, but I did take your advice to heart yesterday and I do want to learn. So which composer is it? I'm embarrassed to say I don't know."

When he didn't answer, she prattled on. "Okay, never mind about the music. I'm here for the meeting with production whenever you're ready. Can't wait to move the process along and see the models in the designs, so let's get the party started."

"The party. Right. Like the night we ran into each other in New York." Ridge turned to face her, adjusted his sunglasses and pressed a button on the remote control in his hand to shut off the music. He didn't have to see Caroline clearly to know that she looked radiant, glowing with the dewy-eyed excitement of a new bride—or, rather, a divorcee who had just reconciled with her loser of an ex-husband. How could she have taken Rick back so quickly? Rick Forrester wasn't worthy of Caroline and yet she'd let him just breeze back into her life—into her *bed*—as if he'd done nothing wrong, as if they'd never broken up, and it was more than mystifying—it was galling. When Donna had placed the call to Caroline's cell phone for him early that morning and Rick had picked up instead, his heart had sunk. And then the guy had taken such pleasure in telling him Caroline couldn't talk because she was in the *shower* and they were running a little behind schedule after their *late night* and they were about to have *breakfast together* ... Well, it disappointed him, to put it mildly. And he had to be honest with himself: it made him jealous.

He had no logical reason to feel jealous, he knew that; jealousy was nonsensical, completely irrational. And yet he hadn't stopped thinking about Caroline since they'd run into each other at Luc's opening, and his preoccupation with her had only grown now she was back at Forrester Creations. From the minute she'd walked into his office, so buoyant and feisty and full of life, it was as if she'd turned on a light switch inside of him. She was so sexy with her high-energy enthusiasm, her clever ideas and her unique ability to understand exactly what he'd been trying to accomplish with his designs. She'd given him a lift, given him someone whose company he actually looked forward to, given him hope that there was happiness for him once he emerged from behind dark glasses and drawn drapes and lonely nights. Until she'd reappeared in LA, he'd lived strictly in his own head, brooding. He had his routine: get driven to work, handle whatever business needed handling, be driven home at the end of the day and sit in the house. By necessity, RJ spent more time with Brooke since the fire—what good was a father who couldn't watch his son play soccer or throw a ball around with him or be the kind of active dad he'd been before the blindness? So he was mostly alone when he wasn't at the office, and his nightly entertainment consisted of listening to music and trying not to descend into self-pity. He didn't want to be one of those poor-me types, not at all. But he did tend to dwell on his loss of vision, on his promise to himself that, should the condition persist, he would not be a burden to anyone, especially not a woman. And then Caroline Spencer gave him something else to think about. He had this crazy romantic notion that when his sight was eventually restored, he'd tell her how he felt about her and she'd admit she'd been feeling the same way and they'd have a future together. Rick wouldn't be happy about it and there would be friction in the family, but Rick wasn't happy about anything and never would be.

"Are you okay, Ridge?" Caroline asked gently, bringing him back to the matters at hand. "Your eyes … are they hurting today?"

Yes, he thought, *they're burning and I can hardly stand it, but what's really burning is the fact that you slept with Rick.* "Everything's just great," he growled. "Have Donna get everybody in here."

*

Caroline thought the meeting went well, except that Ridge barely said a word. He left it to her to make the presentation of the line-up of designs, which she was happy to do if it was helpful to him. She just worried that his lack of engagement in the discussion, his total withdrawal, was about something she'd done, and she couldn't figure out what it could have been. When he left the office after Pam brought him a sandwich for lunch, Caroline grew even more concerned.

"He had a doctor's appointment," Pam said when Caroline asked about his disappearance. Ridge's aunt wore her customary strand of pearls and pastel sweater, her blond hair curled in a style circa 1950. She tended to turn even trivial statements of fact into dramatic bombshells by her over-the-top gestures and theatrical tone.

"That explains it," said Caroline. "The foul mood. He really must be in pain."

"I'm sure," said Pam. "But he was still han-dling business stuff. He asked me to set up calls with some of the top donors that are coming to the fundraiser, so he must be well enough to work from home this afternoon." She smiled and then said suddenly, "Oh, what the heck," and grabbed Caroline in a bear hug.

"What's this for?" Caroline asked with a laugh.

"Not to be nosy," Pam whispered, "but I understand congratulations are in order."

Caroline extricated herself from the hug. "Congratulations for what?"

Pam giggled. "Oh, I get it. So I'm supposed to keep it under wraps until you kids make an announcement. I won't tell anyone, cross my heart and pinky swear." She hooked her little finger through Caroline's in a symbol of secrecy. "But Donna, on the other hand, has very loose lips. I wouldn't trust her to stay quiet for long. She probably told Ridge, since they were the only two here early this morning."

Caroline shook her head at Pam, mystified. "Told Ridge what? What announcement? And why are you congratulating me?"

"Well, not just you, of course. You and Rick," she said. "Congratulations and welcome back to the family."

"I'm sorry, Pam, but I still—"

"Still don't want to everybody to know, I get it. I just have to say that you two were a cute couple the first time and you're a cute couple the second time. Just promise me you'll have a big fancy wedding for number two. No more spur-of-the-moment ceremonies at family holidays."

It dawned on Caroline that Pam and Donna must have heard about her dinner with Rick and assumed it meant more than it actually did—like a second wedding, which was quite a leap.

"I think I understand now," said Caroline with an amused smile. The rumor mill worked overtime at Forrester Creations. "Yes, Rick took me to a lovely restaurant last night. He wants to work things out between us, but for now we're just ... old friends."

"Yeah, right—old friends who spend the night together in a hotel room." Pam nudged Caroline in the ribs and winked at her.

Now Caroline was truly taken aback. "How did you know about that?"

"Like I said, Donna and Ridge were the only two in the office early this morning. Ridge asked Donna to call your cell—something he wanted to talk to you about before the meeting, I guess—and Rick answered your phone and said you were in the shower. We all put two and two together and ... ta da! Another wedding in your future!"

Rick answered my cell? Caroline thought. She did remember hearing a male voice while she was in the shower, but she'd assumed it was—Why would Rick do that? Why would he pick up her phone unless ... unless he saw Ridge's name on the caller ID screen and decided to stick it to his least favorite person by overinflating his importance in Caroline's life? Or was he marking his territory because Ridge had claimed her as his co-designer and had demanded so much of her time since she'd come back to Forrester Creations? There was no use speculating on what Rick's motivation was, but the fact that he didn't tell her about the call, not even when they were discussing the fashion show, was troubling. Maybe he just forgot to tell her—a small lapse—but if he was all about honesty this time around, he had a funny way of showing it.

A larger question formed in Caroline's head. Did finding out that Rick had spent the night with her, as innocent as it was, bother Ridge enough to make him treat her so coldly in the meeting and, if so, why? Why would he even care, other than that he thought Rick wasn't good enough for her? It couldn't be more than that, could it?

How would she feel if she heard Ridge was suddenly back together with Brooke or Katie? She had to be honest with herself and admit that Ridge intrigued her. No, it was more than that. He had crept into her consciousness. Even with the beard and scruffy hair, even when he was glowering at her, even when he barked orders at her, he fascinated her, made her want to spend more time with him, be around him. Maybe she'd always felt that way, even before her return to the company, and she'd never acknowledged it, but it was there—that pull, that connection between them. Never did she feel so much pleasure coaxing a smile out of anyone, and when something she said or did elicited a break in his wall of gloom, she felt like celebrating.

There's only one way to find out what's really going on here, she thought. "Pam, you said Ridge would be working from home this afternoon, right?"

"After his doctor's appointment. I'm supposed to take some papers over for him to sign. I do that nowadays—help him with documents. I read them to him and then make sure he puts his signature on the right line. Poor guy. You just know he hates not doing everything himself."

"Tell you what," said Caroline. "I'll take him the papers this afternoon. I have to go over a few details with him from today's meeting, so it's just as easy to do it in person."

"Sure. Why not," said Pam. "And when you're done with business, you can go find Rick and have the night to yourselves, you lovebirds."

Rick. Caroline tried not to let his phone interception rile her. Even if she demanded an explanation, he'd just say he'd taken Ridge's call for her in case it was important and that he'd forgotten to tell her about it. No point in even getting into it with him. Keep the peace and avoid conflict before the fundraiser. That was what mattered. Still, his lack of transparency did not go unnoticed.

Chapter Eight

Caroline was gathering her things and was about to leave for the day when Pam called.

"Eric wants to see you ASAP. Can you stop at the house before you take the documents over to Ridge? He said it's important."

"Of course," said Caroline, who missed seeing Eric around the office. She was sorry to hear he hadn't been well. "Are you sure he's up to having visitors?"

"He's a little weak," said Pam, "and he can't go gallivanting around the world the way he was doing for a while, but he's better. He just has to rest up, watch his diet and take his meds. He really does want to see you. I guess it's about the fashion show. He's supposed to sit this one out, of course, but he's chomping at the bit to be involved. His only contribution will be a speech that he'll write and Thomas will deliver, sort of a dedication to Stephanie and a vote of confidence in Forrester Creations. Since he doesn't know the first thing about computers—he can barely work the remote on his TV—I'm supposed to go over with my trusty digital recorder while he reads the speech for me to transcribe. Maybe he wants you to help him pull it together?"

"Happy to do it," said Caroline.

＊

Eric Forrester, the patriarch of the family and the co-founder of Forrester Creations with his wife Stephanie, had been like a father to Caroline when she was married to Rick and working at the company the first time around. He was always kind to her, generous and caring, a man she revered. He ran the company with fairness as well as firmness, and his designs were legendary. But what really set him apart for her was his ability to skillfully and sensitively handle the temperaments of his two very different sons, Ridge and Rick. Ridge was the product of his enduring marriage to Stephanie, Rick of his more complicated involvement with Brooke, and both men were forever jockeying for the seat of power at the company and the top spot for their father's love—the title of favored son in every way. Now that Eric had stepped back from the day-to-day operations at

Forrester Creations, the seat of power belonged to Ridge, but Rick was obsessed with seizing it for himself and their acrimony was a source of anguish for Eric.

"Looking lovely as ever," he said, opening his arms to fold Caroline into a hug as they greeted each other in the living room of the Forrester estate—the house she knew so well, the house in which she and Rick had been married on Thanksgiving Day.

"And you look perfectly healthy to me," Caroline teased, regarding the handsome, distinguished-looking man in the burgundy velvet robe. Women of all ages still fell for his silver hair, wise eyes and dimpled chin, not to mention his courtly charm, and she could certainly see why. "I think you're faking sick so you can stay home and tinkle the keys on that piano all day." She nodded at the gleaming black grand piano where Eric often serenaded the family on special occasions.

"Come. Sit with me." He took her hand and led her over to the sofa by the fireplace, the portrait of the formidable Stephanie Forrester watching over them. "How's it going over at the office so far?"

Caroline filled him in on the designs she and Ridge had settled on, how they'd met with the production team and when she expected to see samples. "I think we'll be right on schedule."

"I had no doubt that you'd whip the place into shape, just the way you and Rick took charge of the Hope for the Future line when it was floundering." He sighed, his smile fading. "It goes without saying that I loved having you as a daughter-in-law and that my younger son behaved badly. I'm sorry about all of that."

"Oh, Eric. You've always been wonderful to me." Caroline gave his hand a squeeze. "My love and respect for you will never change. And speaking of the fundraiser, if you need me to help you write your speech for it, don't hesitate to ask. Pam said she'd be coming over to record you."

"I have plenty of time to pull my thoughts together," he assured her. "It'll just be the CEO Emeritus greeting the guests in absentia, thanking them for their contributions to cancer research and paying tribute to Stephanie—nothing I can't handle."

"So you didn't ask me here this afternoon for a report about the fashion show? Pam was wrong about that?"

"Ah, Pam and her assumptions." He chuckled. "No. I wanted to apologize to you on Rick's behalf and to do it in person. I also wanted to discuss Ridge with you."

"I'm not sure what Rick may have told you—he seems to have given everybody the idea that we're back together," said Caroline. "We had one dinner, that's all. It's a beginning, but I don't know if there's anything there for me anymore. We're a long way from any sort of reconciliation."

"Thank you for being honest," said Eric. "It's for you to decide whether you two have a future together, so let's move on to Ridge. I'm worried about him. I'm worried about him personally and I'm worried about him as our acting CEO. He's disengaged and I can't blame him, after what he's been through and what he's still going through. But I'm hearing rumbles that our important buyers are concerned. We've done what we can to downplay his sight loss in the media, but word is out that he's not running the company with the same fire in his belly and we can't afford to see orders drop. This fundraiser in Stephanie's honor is Forrester Creations' public relations opportunity to show the world that we've still got it—that Ridge is still turning out the iconic designs that made us what we are—and I don't want it to slip through our fingers."

"I'm doing my best to make sure that doesn't happen, Eric. I promise you."

"I know that, Caroline, and I have the utmost confidence in you. But how can we get Ridge to feel better about his life and his work, more hopeful? You've spent the past couple of days with him. Have there been hints of the old Ridge? Any ideas how to bring him around? You seem to know how to do just about everything, so I thought I'd ask."

Caroline considered Eric's questions. "He's been angry, moody—distant."

"So everybody tells me." Eric nodded ruefully. "My oldest son can be gruff and bullheaded even under the best of circumstances, but he's got a huge heart when he likes someone, and he likes you, Caroline. He must like you because you're the only designer he didn't say no to when we were all begging him to bring in help for the fashion show."

"I like him too, Eric. Not when he's growling at me but when he does let me in, he can be very …" Caroline trailed off as she flashed back to the night at Luc's, to the sensation of Ridge's fingers lingering on her lips, of the way he'd looked at her …

Eric arched an eyebrow. "I have a feeling this collaboration of yours is going better than I anticipated."

"It is," she confirmed. "I mean it's only been a couple of days, but I think I'm getting through—a little."

"Then maybe you'll come up with some way to draw him out, show him that he's still important, not only to the company but also to all of us who care about him—drag him out of the house at the very least. It would be good for him and good for Forrester Creations."

"You want me to help him psychologically?" she said, making sure she understood. "I'm not a shrink, Eric."

"What I'm asking, if you're willing, is for you to apply your considerable cleverness and personal magnetism to Ridge in a way that will boost his morale, make him feel that there's a reason to get up in the morning. There must be some way you can do that. I've seen what a spitfire you are. I remember how you stuck your own neck out for Rick time and time again and how you weren't a bit afraid to take on Ridge in the process." He smiled. "I know this is beyond the job description; we brought you out here to design dresses, after all. I'm just asking as a favor. Use the spitfire in you to get Ridge to open up a little, since he likes and respects you. Let him know he's not diminished as a leader, as a human being, as a *man*. If an idea how to do that comes to you, I'll be very grateful."

Caroline did light on an idea and it made perfect sense to her. Her idea would be a way for Ridge to feel like a boss and mentor again, to escape his own dark thoughts, a way for Forrester Creations to have a CEO who realized he was much more than a pair of damaged eyes. It would also be a way for her to have some fun while she was in LA—a win-win for everybody.

"You've thought of something?" Eric asked. "You look like I used to whenever I'd hit on an idea for a new design."

"Yes, I just might have!" said Caroline. "I'm due over at Ridge's as soon as I leave here and I'll try it out on him."

"Sounds promising," said Eric. "Just one more thing: Ridge can't know that I asked you to intervene, so this conversation needs to stay between us. I don't think he'd take it well if he thought his father was meddling in either his personal or professional life. Understood?"

"Of course, but I genuinely want to help him and Forrester Creations," Caroline assured him, "even if you hadn't asked me to."

"You're one in a million, you know that?" They rose from the sofa and Eric wrapped her in another hug before walking her to the door. "Oh. One more caveat," he said before sending her on her way. "Rick is sensitive—overly sensitive, if you ask me—if it looks like I'm showing Ridge any sort of favoritism or extra attention, and it would be detrimental to the company, as well as hurtful to him, if he thought I'd asked you to spend more of your time with Ridge ... Look, all I'm saying is that however you decide to accomplish our goal for Ridge, try to keep my sons from going to war over you—at least until after the fundraiser."

"Over me?" Caroline was taken aback by Eric's remark until she remembered Rick's use of the very same words just the night before. Still, a war over her seemed highly unlikely.

Eric shrugged. "Who knows why two people develop a connection, but it happens and that's life and there's nothing wrong with it. All I'm saying is that Forrester Creations needs this event to go off without a hitch, so tread carefully."

*

Ridge lived in the Bel Air section of LA amid movie stars and captains of industry and families with old money. He'd bought the house, a gated, Tuscan-style estate nestled just up the road from the famed Bel Air Hotel, when he'd returned from Paris to settle into Forrester Creations as its new CEO. He'd hoped it would be the ideal home for RJ whenever his custody arrangement with Brooke allowed for visits. There were plenty of bedrooms for the boy and his friends, and the Bel Air Country Club was nearby if his son ever decided to trade soccer for golf. He'd had no idea that the house's location would end up being a godsend for him too; his old friend Jerome, the concierge at the Bel Air Hotel, took it upon himself to find Ridge a suitable attendant, a young waiter from the hotel dining room named Ben, who brought meals and helped with everyday tasks that were difficult for Ridge to manage on his own. Ben arrived first thing in the morning, helped him get ready for work and came back at the end of the day to check on him. It was a practical setup and Ridge was grateful for Ben's efficient yet unobtrusive demeanor, but he longed for the day when he didn't need an attendant and could get back to leading a normal life.

Unfortunately, that day would not be soon; his doctor's appointment had not gone as Ridge had hoped, and Dr Connolly was puzzled by the lingering red spots and dark shadows that still obscured his patient's vision.

"The pigment layer in the eyes, or RPE, has numerous metabolic and immune system functions," said the ocular specialist. "As you know, your exposure to the intense light of the fire decreased the pigment, Ridge, but it should have regenerated by now."

"Then why the hell hasn't it?" Ridge demanded and immediately apologized for his outburst.

"I know it's been a rough road." Dr Connolly placed his hand on Ridge's shoulder to steady him. "As I've explained, one function of the pigment is to protect the underlying retinal cells, which are part of the nervous system, from excessive light. Blindness—including the partial blindness you're experiencing now—persists until the RPE is fully regenerated. In your case, I suppose it's conceivable that the nervous system itself is to blame."

"The nervous system? Are you saying if I just relax and enjoy myself I'll be cured?"

"No, not at all, although anything that reduces stress—learning deep-breathing techniques, doing some low-impact exercise like yoga, engaging in activities that help take your mind off your condition—wouldn't hurt. But the nervous system is a difficult beast to tame and sometimes we doctors have to act counter-intuitively. Which is to say, we do nothing and let it right itself."

Ridge shook his head with incredulity. "So there's no pill, no treatment, nothing else you can do? I'm just supposed to wait this thing out—while I'm contorting myself into some yoga position?"

"That's exactly what I'm telling you. I can give you more medication for the pain and I suggest you continue to limit your light exposure whenever possible, but other than that, my friend, you need to find a way to be patient and let this resolve on its own. I promise you it will."

"Are you staking your reputation on that promise, Dr Connolly?"

"I am, Ridge—unequivocally. I just can't say when."

*

Pam had given Caroline the gate code for Ridge's house as well as the key so he wouldn't have to stumble around to let her in. Not that he knew she was coming. She'd decided to show up unannounced instead of calling ahead to say that she, not Pam, would be bringing the documents for him to sign. Given his frostiness at the meeting, she didn't want to risk having him insist that she not come.

Her driver pulled up to the house, set high atop its own private knoll with an unobstructed, panoramic view of the Pacific Ocean and Catalina Island over a canopy of greenery. Caroline actually gasped as she took in the beauty surrounding her. She'd grown up a child of privilege at one of the best addresses in Manhattan—a city girl whose parents' historic townhouse sat proudly on the Upper East Side. But this—this magnificent eyeful of the sea and the sky and the trees along with the soaring feeling of being on top of the world—was so spectacular that she bounded out of the limo and stood on the front lawn for several minutes, absorbing it all.

It was only after the limo left the driveway that she was reminded of the reason she'd come. Clutching the envelope containing the documents for Ridge to sign, she let herself in his front door. She stepped into the striking entrance hall where more grandeur awaited her—not the sort of gaudy opulence she'd seen inside some of the mansions of LA but a home befitting the CEO of one of the world's most prestigious fashion houses.

She walked past the double staircase and into the formal living room, observing every detail as she went: the beamed ceiling, the mahogany floor, the imported rugs, the tasteful furnishings. The heavy draperies were drawn but she pulled one back to take a quick peek through the French doors that led to an expansive patio and beyond, to the sparkling infinity pool and lush landscaping. She continued her tour of the room with its silver-framed photos and fine antiques, and her overall impression was old-world elegance meets modern glamor with a hint of whimsy; along with the state-of-the-art lighting and electronic equipment, there was an old-fashioned pinball machine tucked into a corner. Caroline smiled as she guessed there were similar playful touches throughout the house, perhaps for RJ's benefit, perhaps for his father's.

"Pam?"

Caroline turned. Ridge had been expecting his aunt, of course. "It's Caroline, Ridge," she said, walking toward him. "I hope it's all right. I stopped by with those papers Pam needs you to sign."

"I should have recognized the footsteps," he said coolly. "Yours bounce."

She wasn't sure whether to take that as a compliment or not.

"I didn't know you ran errands along with your other talents," he said.

So we're back to the sarcasm, she thought with a keen sense of disappointment. He had been so engaged the day before when he was asking her about herself, so warm—for him. And now there was this … chill. Was it because of his doctor's appointment or Rick's deliberate mention of their night together?

She asked if they could sit down.

"Sorry. My manners again." Ridge motioned for her to follow him into another room. It was too big to be called a den, more like a study or library. It had wall-to-wall bookcases, a leather-top desk and an entertainment center with the latest flat-screen TV, DVD player and speakers. Caroline sat on the loveseat. Ridge maneuvered himself over to his desk chair.

"Should we get the business over with first?" she asked, removing the documents from the envelope. "Pam said you've already gone over the contracts with legal, and these are just the executed copies for your signature."

"By all means," he said, waving her over to him.

She didn't know how much he could see. With the plantation shutters closed, the room was fairly dark except for the lamp at the end of the desk, and then there was his limited vision. Pam had flagged the lines where he was supposed to sign his name, but maybe he still needed help.

Caroline drew closer so she could stand over his shoulder as she laid the papers in front of him and flipped them open to the appropriate pages. "Here's a pen," she said, reaching for the one nearby and literally inserting it between the thumb and forefinger of his right hand.

He smirked. "I think I could have picked up my own pen, but thanks." With Caroline's guidance, Ridge signed the required pages and handed them back to her. "Was that really worth the trip over here or was there something else you wanted?" he asked.

Caroline sat back down on the loveseat and considered the question. Should she explain about the mix up with Rick? Discussing her personal life was presuming an awful lot. Maybe the great and powerful Ridge Forrester didn't care a bit who was romancing her and who wasn't and that blabbing to him about Rick's phone faux pas, the shower and the rest of it would only annoy him. Better not to mention it at all, she decided. Besides, she had something more positive to discuss: her plan for lifting his spirits. She'd come up with it at the end of her meeting with Eric and honed it during the drive to Bel Air, and now was the time to see if it would fly with Ridge.

"There's definitely something else I want," she said, becoming excited as she spoke but trying not to bounce on her seat cushion. "Please hear me out before you answer and please keep an open mind, okay?"

"I have a feeling this isn't about a design for the fashion show."

"It's about me getting out of the bubble. You talked about that yesterday, remember? You gave me an assignment to get out of the bubble?"

"As I've said, Caroline, it's my eyesight that's bad. My memory's just fine."

"Right. You also said that I didn't need to work on the fashion show twenty-four-seven and I agree. It's in the production team's lap now and until we see the dresses on the models, there will be gaps in our schedules."

"*Our* schedules? I have a company to run." Ridge stroked his beard as he regarded her from behind his dark glasses.

"Yes, but—well, just let me finish." She took a breath. Sometimes she got so wound up about an idea that she tended to gulp her words. "I'd like you to take me out of the bubble, be my tour guide, in a way. What I mean is that there are interests outside of fashion I'd like to explore, the way you suggested, and you're just the person to facilitate it. For example, when I came into your office earlier today, you were listening to classical music. I couldn't tell if you were listening to Bach or Beethoven or someone I've never heard of, so teach me. Another example: You mentioned that I should go see a sports team. I want you to take me to a stadium or a ballpark or whatever you call those places and explain what I'm watching. You also mentioned that I should seek out food trucks and other alternatives to the fancy places around here and savor the exotic flavors. I want you to do that with me so I'll learn the difference between curry and cumin. And I want to dance, Ridge. Not ballroom dance or ballet dance but go to a concert with a dance floor and get up and shake it, really cut loose like I've never done before. One of those blues bands where the lead singer sounds like he's straight out of a gospel choir would be perfect.

"The point is, I want you to help me with this mission just like I'm helping you with the fashion show."

*

Ridge sat back in his chair and marveled at her, at the miracle of her. Who was this woman, this beautiful young creature who vibrated with a kind of dynamism he'd never seen in anyone—a woman who'd suddenly become the only ray of light to penetrate his darkness? He'd heard people ramble about things happening for a reason and he'd always thought it was just a bunch of New Age mumbo jumbo, but he was beginning to wonder if the reason for his blindness, as traumatic as it had been for him, was to bring Caroline Spencer back into his life. And then there was the fact that he wanted her and probably had since that night at Luc's. There was no denying the attraction she held for him. He wanted her with every part of him—mind, body and soul. He wanted her energy and her creativity and her light—and yes, he wanted her voluptuousness, her ripeness. He hadn't been with a woman since the fire—and for some time even before then; he hadn't felt that sort of charged connection with anybody enough to make the effort. But Caroline wasn't just anybody. He knew that now.

"I'm flattered that you took my suggestions seriously," he said after clearing his throat so he wouldn't betray his desire. "But has it escaped you that I can't see very well and that my poor eyesight might put a damper on your trip to, say, the ballpark? I can't explain the mechanics of a sport I can't watch."

"Not true at all," Caroline asserted. "How about we go to a hockey game? We'll sit right down near the ice and one of the players will hit the ball with the bat and—"

"The 'ball' is called a puck," said Ridge with a grin. "And the 'bat' is a stick."

Caroline smiled. "You see? You taught me a couple of things already and we haven't even gone yet. As I was saying, we'll sit there and they'll score touchdowns and you'll tell me—"

"Goals," he said, laughing outright. "They're called goals."

"I'm more convinced than ever that this will be great—a terrific learning experience for me—and it'll get you out of the house," she said. "Which is amazing. Your house, I mean."

"I'm glad you like it. You'll have to stop by again."

"Oh, I'll be back—for my music lesson. And after we cross that off the list, we'll tackle the other items and they'll entail field trips. I'll research the wheres and whens, we'll get Pam or Donna to clear our schedules and my driver will take us to our destinations. Done deal?"

He didn't answer. He honestly didn't know what to say. Her idea was enticing and yet completely unworkable. While it was true that there were pockets of time in his schedule, even with the fundraiser looming, and that his nights were always free, it was preposterous to think he could manage the activities she was proposing, not with red spots clouding his vision. And his eyes were still sensitive to bright lights, although he supposed if he wore the dark glasses and a baseball cap with a good-sized bill he'd be protected enough. He allowed himself to be swept up in her nearness and enthusiasm. The sweet scent of her perfume and the melodic sound of her voice were a tonic for him, no matter how badly he wanted to resist. He could hear the rustling of her dress, even the tinkling of her earrings, and he wished he could see her, not just in some odd mosaic of images, but all of her—with crystal clarity. But what good was any of it? He was damaged goods and she belonged to Rick.

"Come on," Caroline urged. "You're my boss, so it makes perfect sense that you'd be my coach too."

"Your boss," he said. "You're the one who does the bossing, if you ask me. Are you always like this?"

"Like what?"

"So determined to get your way?"

She smiled. "When I want something badly enough. Part of this assignment is to get me out of the bubble, but the other part is to get you out of your comfort zone. The man I ran into in New York wouldn't be hiding behind a desk, Ridge."

"The man you ran into in New York had twenty-twenty vision."

"Maybe, but since you keep bragging about your memory, do you remember what you said to me that night? I do. You said using *all* the senses—sight, hearing, smell, feel and taste—was the key to enjoying life to the fullest."

"I said that, huh? What a pompous ass."

"That too," she said, "but it's true, Ridge. Losing your sight was a serious blow, but it'll come back and in the meantime, you've still got the other senses. Don't neglect them."

How did she get so wise at such a young age? Wise and beautiful, smart and sexy—and funny. Yes, funny. She made him laugh at a time when no one else could, even when she was mocking him. "Fine," he said. "You win. I don't know how this scheme of yours could possibly work, but I'll do it." She was impossible to say no to, he'd discovered.

Caroline bounced up and down on the loveseat cushion. "You won't be sorry," she said.

"What about Rick?"

"What about him?"

"Rumor has it that you two are back together—and so quickly. Won't he mind you spending non-business hours with me?"

"Number one: don't believe everything you hear. Number two: I came to LA to make sure the fundraiser goes smoothly. I intend to fulfill that promise, and if it means keeping the peace between you and Rick then that's what I'll do—whatever it takes. Let's leave it at that."

"Fair enough."

Chapter Nine

The following week, Caroline juggled her work at Forrester Creations with another dinner with Rick as well as an outing with Ridge—without either of them knowing about the other. Her friend Gigi was totally spot-on when she'd warned Caroline that she'd be walking right smack into the middle of the forever-battling Forrester brothers by returning to LA.

Rick was waging a nonstop campaign to win Caroline back—from the evening out at yet another romantic, insanely expensive restaurant (this time he'd arranged to have her serenaded by a trio of operatic waiters and a violinist) to the daily delivery to her hotel of a single sunflower for her breakfast tray. He was sweet. He was solicitous. And he was eager for some sign from her that he was winning her over. For her part,

Caroline was careful not to promise too much or string him along or seem duplicitous in any way at the same time as she was also careful to express her gratitude for his attention, keep an open mind about him and give them at least a chance for a reconciliation. He still meant something to her, of that there was no doubt, but she didn't know exactly what. Were her feelings those of nostalgia for what they'd once been as a couple, a reflex borne out of habit and history? Or were they real in the moment and an indication that her love for him was still there, the embers buried under the hurt and mistrust but still flickering? She didn't know and, she reminded herself, she didn't need to know. Not yet. She had just over a month to see the fundraiser to its conclusion before having to decide whether she'd stay in LA or go home, and she intended to take every bit of that time to process her feelings, ticking clock or not.

As for Ridge, her own campaign to provide entertaining distractions for him and make him feel whole again, let him see that he had value in spite of his sight loss, show him he should take his own advice and use all his senses for a full life, didn't get off to a promising start.

She'd decided to take him to Staples Center in downtown LA for a hockey game since he'd suggested she introduce herself to the world of professional sports. The LA Kings were playing the Arizona Coyotes and she'd bought two tickets. It was at the last minute, so the premier section down in front near the ice rink was sold out, and they had to sit way up in the stands, wedged between two very beefy, very drunk groups of fans. Staples Center had an elevator, which was helpful in getting them to the Upper Concourse, but Ridge had refused to allow Caroline to arrange for a wheelchair or a special escort—"My legs are just fine," he'd reminded her—so walking him to their row and guiding him to their seats was arduous. He'd tripped numerous times, stepped on toes and, just as he was settling into his seat, moved his elbow onto the armrest he shared with a large man clutching a large cup of beer, collided with the cup and quickly found his lap soaked with the man's Bud Lite.

"I'm so sorry," Caroline must have said a thousand times as she swabbed frantically at his jeans with a wad of napkins. "I promise I'll plan better next time."

"I can hardly wait."

Had he actually smiled when he said that? Caroline asked herself. Yes, he had, and she was overjoyed, relieved too. He'd been a good sport in spite of her miscalculations and she was grateful.

"Besides, I like having you clean me up," he'd added with the faintest hint of a laugh. "I feel like a toddler with an overturned bowl of applesauce. Perhaps I should have worn a full-body bib."

"You're being a very sweet toddler. No tantrums," she'd said and threaded her arm through his, as if it were the most natural gesture in the world.

When the game got underway, Caroline had asked Ridge to explain the basics of what was going on. Why were there red and blue lines on the ice? How many players were on each team and what was their function? Why did they fight so much? Every time Ridge had tried to answer her questions, the drunks on either side of them had drowned him out. He'd been remarkably good-natured about it all, Caroline thought, even cracking a joke: "They're loud enough to make me deaf *and* blind."

Caroline had really enjoyed his story about growing up rooting for the Detroit Red Wings. The Kings were a mostly mediocre team when he was a kid and the Red Wings were the best, he'd said, and told her how he'd idolized a Russian superstar named Sergei Federov, how Americans didn't appreciate hockey the way fans did in countries like Canada, Russia and Scandinavia and how he and father had taken the Forrester jet to see the Red Wings win the Stanley Cup in 1997. But their drunk and disorderly seatmates had made real conversation nearly impossible.

At one point, Caroline had left Ridge to buy them food at the concession stand. She came back with two hot dogs and two beers, figuring that since sandwiches were easy for him to manage at meal times, he'd have no problem with the arena's so-called "Skyscraper Dog," which was simply an extra-long frank on which she'd spread mustard, ketchup and relish. She'd handed him the container with the hot dog and placed his beer cup on the floor in front of his seat—only to have him inadvertently knock the beer over with his foot, drenching his shoes.

Worse for Ridge, the lights flashing on the scoreboard, combined with the glare coming off the ice, had inflamed his eyes and though he'd tried not to show it, Caroline had been able to tell he was in pain, despite the protective cap and glasses.

"Let's go. This was a boneheaded idea," she'd said when she realized that he was too polite—or too macho, she didn't know which—to admit they should head for the exit.

"You sure?" Ridge had asked. "It's only the second period. There are three, by the way, unless they go into overtime."

There had been a roar from the crowd and the announcer on the PA system yelled, "Score!"

"What happened?" Ridge had shouted over the din to the neighbor to his left.

"Kopitar scored a goal," said the man. "Kings up by one!"

He high-fived Ridge and for a brief moment, Caroline had thought, the night was saved from being a complete disaster. The look on Ridge's face was pure bliss, like a little boy getting a red fire truck for Christmas.

"Anze Kopitar is their center from Slovenia," he'd told her. "He's not Wayne Gretzky but he's good."

"Who's Wayne Gretzky?" she'd asked, thrilled to see him so energized despite all that had gone wrong.

He'd thrown his head back and laughed with such unadulterated pleasure that she hadn't even minded that it was at her expense. "He's the Babe Ruth of hockey," he'd informed her. "And don't ask who Babe Ruth is."

"I know who *he* is," she'd sniffed. "I'm from New York, remember? He had a candy bar named after him."

"Among his other accomplishments." Ridge had smiled as she reached for his hand and helped him up.

Thinking about the evening now, Caroline took a mental inventory of how her first effort had gone. In the negative column were the bright lights, the placement of their seats and the difficulty of maneuvering Ridge around the enormous arena. On the plus side were his love for the game, the fact that the home team won, his interest in teaching her about the sport and, most importantly, his willingness to step out of his comfort zone. She was determined that their next adventure would go more smoothly.

*

"You are cordially invited to your own house for dinner tonight," Caroline announced to Ridge two weeks after the hockey game, placing her hand on his shoulder. Ridge warmed whenever she made physical contact, and all aggravations dissipated for him. She was the opposite of a cool blond. She was a toucher, demonstrative and spontaneous and at ease with her body, whether it meant giving him a poke in the ribs or a gentle rub on his shoulder. Nothing about her actions felt rehearsed or designed to elicit a specific response, nothing felt premeditated. And he loved when she was near him. He inhaled the cloud of her perfume, the scent that reminded him of how beautiful she was at Luc's that night when he'd last seen her clearly. He ached to hold her now and couldn't, not when he was incapable of getting safely into a seat at a hockey game and not when her heart belonged to Rick, who needled him about her at every opportunity. Only that morning, his half-brother had bragged that he'd made a reservation at some swanky resort in Mexico for him and Caroline—"a possible surprise honeymoon for after the fundraiser." Rick was full of surprises, most of them deceitful and cowardly, Ridge grumbled to himself, but if Rick was what Caroline Spencer really wanted in a man, Ridge wasn't in a position to stand in her way. In the meantime, he'd go along with this Pygmalion routine she'd cooked up for him. Being around her was better than not being around her, even if he did have to keep his desire for her in check.

They were in his office alone after getting a production status report from Thomas and Hope, and the atmosphere was easier, more relaxed, between them now. Not that he didn't snap at her on occasion the way he snapped at the others, but for the most part they had crossed over into a territory that was somewhere between a cordial business relationship and an actual friendship, and he was enjoying it. "May I ask what the occasion is?" said Ridge, perking up at the thought of spending another evening with Caroline, of having her all to himself whether Rick liked it or not.

"My continuing education," she said. "One of the interests I'd like to explore is cooking, so I'm planning to cook you dinner. It'll be in your own deluxe abode, so you won't have to worry about crowds or lights or me falling asleep on you." Their outing the week before had been to the LA Philharmonic at the Walt Disney Hall. She'd wanted him to teach her about classical music and she'd asked the concierge at the Beverly Wilshire Hotel to arrange the tickets this time, the best seats in the house. But after twenty minutes of Beethoven's 6th Symphony, which Ridge had touted as one of the composer's most important works, her head had lolled back and dangled from her shoulders as she'd drifted off into some peaceful netherworld.

"You certainly have me curious," said Ridge of her invitation. "But—and correct me if I'm wrong—I don't picture you with a whisk in your hand, elbow deep in pastry dough, anymore than I pictured you with a beer at the Kings game."

"See that? You have these preconceptions of people, Ridge."

"No, just of you, Caro."

"Caro? Is that my new nickname?" she asked with a wry smile. "Or is it the name of one of your tragic Italian operas I don't know anything about?"

He laughed. "You mocking me again?"

"Yes. You're very mockable."

Ridge adored when she poked fun at him. It suggested there was something personal and intimate between them, a language only the two of them spoke with each other, something not even his dim vision could take away, and it made their chemistry, their connection, that much more charged—at least for him. "The name 'Caro' just came to me," he said. "It's spunky, feisty, a little offbeat, like you—a woman who dresses in Forrester Creations couture but downs beer and Skyscraper Dogs. 'Caroline' was more fitting for your aunt. She was so lovely, but she glided into a room—you bounce into it."

"Right. I forgot you think I bounce. So how's tonight? Is your calendar free?"

"I'll have to cancel the sixteen other dinner invites waiting for my RSVP, but sure. Just don't give me stomach poisoning, Caro. I've got enough to deal with."

*

Caroline went straight to Ridge's favorite chef for inspiration: Luc Bergeron, whose first cookbook sounded the least intimidating of the three he'd published. Not that Caroline had ever prepared a French dinner for two; her idea of cooking was stopping for takeout at one of Manhattan's gourmet food emporiums and then reheating it in the microwave when she got home. Although she had felt ambitious at Thanksgiving one year and decided she would make the turkey. The recipe said to wash it inside and out, and she had taken the directions literally, dousing it in lemon-scented dishwashing liquid. The result had been a soap-infused bird. Since then, she'd watched a couple of cooking shows on television and was intrigued by the challenge of combining flavors for a delicious meal. Luc's recipe for sea scallops with potato puree and onion confit seemed like the perfect way to go. The scallops would be in small pieces and, hopefully, easy for Ridge to spear with his fork, and the puree was basically mashed potatoes and how hard could they be for her to make and him to eat? She had no idea what confit was but she'd figure it out.

Her limo took her to the market to buy all the ingredients. Then it was up to Bel Air, where she met Ridge's attendant, Ben, at the house so he could show her around the kitchen and help her locate the necessary pots and pans. And then she was on her own.

She peeled all the potatoes, a thankless job she didn't care to repeat, and then boiled them in a big pot of water. The recipe said to drain them after twenty minutes and mash them through a sieve or food mill. Ridge didn't have a sieve or food mill. "Such a nuisance," Caroline sniffed as she opened drawers and cabinets searching for equipment about which she didn't have a clue.

Fine, I'll use a fork, she thought, and spent nearly an hour trying to mash a pound of potatoes with the lone utensil. Her hand cramped and her arm ached and she was so frustrated when she stared down at the lumpy potatoes that she doubled the heavy cream and butter the recipe called for and dumped them into the pot. The end product was soup. Lumpy, cold, potato soup.

The scallops were supposed to be cooked at the very last minute before serving, so Caroline waited until Ridge came home to deal with them. She greeted him, brought him a glass of wine, set the table in the dining room and hurried back into the kitchen to finish up.

She dredged the scallops in flour and stuck them in a hot skillet with the rest of the ingredients. They were supposed to cook for only four minutes, but she was distracted by the confit, which she'd completely forgotten about.

Okay, they're just onions, she thought, rereading the recipe. *I'm supposed to "sweat" them in butter and balsamic vinegar until they're caramelized. Does that mean they should turn the color of caramel candy?*

While she waited for the onions to look like caramel, the scallops were morphing into shoe leather. Or maybe small white hockey pucks was more like it. She sighed as she poured them over the lumpy potato soup and onions. The white blobs upon more white blobs in her dish did not look like the photo in Luc's cookbook, not at all.

"Smells great," said Ridge as she carried the dish into the dining room, her mood as funereal as though she were carrying a body in a casket. "What are we having, if I may be allowed to ask?"

"Vichyssoise."

"Chilled potato soup?"

"You got it."

Caroline slumped down in her chair next to Ridge's and pouted. As he fumbled for his spoon and began to bring the food to his mouth to taste it, she grabbed his arm.

Hilary Rose

"Don't! It's like wet cement."

He laughed. "Bad as all that?"

"It is and I'm sorry. I'm failing miserably at broadening my horizons. How can you be my coach if I don't give you anything to work with?"

Ridge reached for her face and held her cheek in his sturdy yet graceful right hand, the hand that had conceived the dresses of the world's most fashionable women—the hand that had caressed the faces of the world's most beautiful women too. "You're very hard on yourself, you know that?" he said.

"You're hard on yourself too, Ridge," she said, her body vibrating from his touch. It had been so unexpected and yet, if she was really honest with herself, it was a natural extension of the warmth and playfulness that had developed between them and, yes, of the sexual energy between them. She'd always known her attraction for him was there, even when they were sparring, even when it was lurking underneath all the harsh words. They were both passionate people. And now she was giving in to that passion as his fingertips danced across her cheek and the heat rose up from every part of her. What was it about being near him that fired her up, made her feel so alive, so desirous? Why did every single cell in her body pulsate whenever she came within a few feet of him? Was it the conquest, the challenge of ensnaring the great and powerful Ridge Forrester? No, she

134

wasn't the kind of woman who attached herself to a man just because he had money and prestige; if that were true she wouldn't have fallen in love with Rick when he was struggling at Forrester Creations and searching for his place in the company.

"All I was trying to do tonight was lighten your burdens. I can't even feed you properly."

"Nonsense. I'm hardly malnourished. I thought one of the purposes of these activities was for me to expose you to new things," he said. "Since you tell me this dinner isn't worth salvaging, why don't we get the hell out of here and have some real food?"

Caroline brightened, thrilled that it was Ridge who was suggesting they venture out of his safety zone for a change. "At one of those off-the-beaten-path places you mentioned?"

"If you promise not to fall asleep on me. Grab that nice bottle of wine you brought and let's beat it."

Chapter Ten

Ridge took Caroline on what he called a "Strip Crawl." And he wasn't talking about Hollywood's famous Sunset Strip or a string of girlie lap dance clubs. He advised her limo driver that they were heading for East LA.

"I assume this is new territory for you," he said to Caroline, who was staring out the window during the drive like Alice in Wonderland peering through the looking glass. They were whizzing past empty parking lots, abandoned buildings, convenience stores and modest houses with tidy lawns and children's swing sets. "Not Beverly Hills or Bel Air, is it?"

"A whole different LA for me," she agreed.

He was tempted to put his hand on her knee. He was still ignited by the way he'd touched her cheek earlier, couldn't stop thinking about it, just as he couldn't forget when he'd brushed his fingers across her lips at Luc's party. Touching Caroline at last, expressing the tenderness he'd felt toward her, allowing himself the pleasure of making contact with her flesh, had nearly overwhelmed Ridge and it had been all he could do not to move closer and press his lips against hers, crush his body against hers. His attraction for her was like a wave that kept rising and rising and threatening to swallow him whole. "It's a real neighborhood, as in real people," he said. "Lots of young families and working class folks who've been priced out of the high-ticket areas you see on the pretty postcards with all the glitter and palm trees. Not the Forrester Creations couture market, in other words."

Soon they arrived at a street that was dotted with Mom and Pop stores as well as a row of food trucks—a "strip," hence Ridge's name for their jaunt.

"What's our first stop?" asked the limo driver.

Ridge gave the driver the name of one of the trucks and turned to Caroline. "Have you ever eaten goat?"

"Goat, as in 'baaaah?'"

He laughed. "That's sheep—goats make a sound like 'maaaaah,' which is close. You would know that if you'd gone to a petting zoo when you were a kid."

"Obviously, I led a deprived childhood. But to answer your question, no, I've never eaten goat. Why?"

"Because you're about to."

With help from Caroline, Ridge made his way over to the truck and conversed in fluent Spanish with the Mexican man at the order window, who explained that his parents had a similar birria stand in Nochistlan, Zacatecas and that cooking was a source of both income and family pride. Within minutes, he handed Ridge a hearty helping of piping hot roasted goat meat smothered in onions and spices and wrapped in a tortilla.

"I figured we should share," he said, feeding Caroline the first bite, "since we'll be making several stops and we need to pace ourselves."

Caroline sank her teeth into the moist and juicy tortilla and moaned with pleasure. "Oh my God. This is totally delicious and I don't even care that the sauce is dribbling down my chin. Tastes like lamb, only richer, stronger."

"Best goat around," Ridge agreed, savoring his bite. "Are you getting all the flavors of the spices?"

"Oh yeah," she said, taking her time chewing every morsel. "It all transports me to some exotic place. I'll tell you right now—you can't get anything like this in New York."

"Sure you can," said Ridge. "When you get home, hop on the subway and take a ride to the Jamaican part of the city. You'll get incredible curried goat there."

"I've never taken the subway anywhere," she said. "And I didn't know we had a Jamaican section in New York."

"It's called getting out of the bubble, Caro."

"What if I decide not to go home at all?" she said teasingly. "Not that anyone's asked me to stay," she clarified, realizing she'd put him on the spot. "Well, I mean Rick has, but—"

"I'd rather not bring Rick into the discussion if it's all the same to you."

Caroline went silent, and he wished she hadn't mentioned his brother's name—it had cast a temporary pall over the otherwise lighthearted evening. He didn't want to think about how she'd gone back to Rick and how these outings were nothing more than him helping Caroline explore the wider world.

"Here we are," said Ridge when they'd arrived at their next destination, a truck serving up a deep-fried corn taco stuffed with shrimp and enveloped in a fiery tomato salsa.

"Oh! Oh! Oh!" said Caroline, her eyes watering from the peppery heat of the salsa. "This should be illegal. The shrimp is so succulent. It explodes in your mouth, doesn't it? And the taco is so freshly made I can practically smell it coming out of the fryer, and it provides just the right amount of crunch and texture, like a chip."

"That it does." He nodded at her approvingly. "Listen to you, going all poetic about the food. Using all your senses too, am I right?"

"Aren't you always?"

He laughed. "Pretty much."

I'm laughing again, Ridge thought. *She's made me laugh and I'm enjoying myself. She may be getting out of the bubble, but I'm getting out of the darkness too.*

It was onto more trucks and their specialties, from sushi burritos, Korean barbecued short rib tacos and lobster slathered with extra-garlicky aioli in a split bun to the best buttermilk Southern fried chicken Caroline said she'd ever tasted. Topping off the tour was the truck that was scooping out artisanal ice cream.

"I feel like I've just died and gone to heaven," said Caroline, as she patted her full belly on the drive back to Bel Air. "My mouth is still talking to me."

"What's it saying?" He could see how satiated, how secure she felt in the back seat of the limo, where the privacy screen provided an almost cocoon-like atmosphere, as though Caroline and he were the only two people alive.

"Take a closer look. At my mouth, I mean," she said invitingly.

He was emboldened by the heat of the food and the rush of experiencing wonderful things with someone he would never have considered spending even five minutes with before she'd made it her mission to know him better. This night, like all of their nights, wasn't about any promise Caroline had made to Forrester

Creations; it was strictly about her and Ridge, about his growing attraction to her. He couldn't deny it, didn't want to deny it—or resist it. He was never one to sit around passively waiting; he felt something for her—and it wasn't purely professional—and he needed to act.

As he leaned in, his face nearly touching hers, Caroline removed his sunglasses. He tried not to show how she'd startled him by taking away his protection, his barricade against the lights, the elements, the pitying expressions of others, but he didn't grab them back. It was dark in the limo, as dark as the starless night sky, so he didn't think she'd be hurting his eyes by leaving them bare, not for just a few moments. He let his eyes rest on her face, hoping their vacant appearance, the white part around his iris no longer white but rather a startling reddish-pink, wouldn't repel her.

"Tell me what you see, Ridge," she said softly.

He was overcome by need—a need to banish all obstacles between them: Rick, the fundraiser, the blindness, the glasses; all of it. He didn't want anything to come between him and this woman who stirred his passion in a way that he'd never have anticipated.

"I see spots and shadows," he said solemnly, his damaged eyes searching her clear ones, her nose, her cheekbones and her mouth before roaming across the rest of her. He broke into a smile. "But—what do you know—I can make out a hint of pistachio ice cream in the left corner of your lower lip."

They both laughed. "I left it there just to test your vision," Caroline joked. "But seriously, it was the most incredible ice cream ever. You're not going to let it go to waste, are you?" She was daring him to do more than look at her.

Ridge accepted the challenge, holding her face in his hands and bringing it toward his, and then he licked the ice cream off her luscious, pouty lip. Hearing her slight intake of breath, her gasp of desire, aroused him even more and he kissed her—hard.

"I've wanted to do that since I saw you in New York," he murmured, before kissing her again. Her body yielded to him, arching toward him, beckoning him to do more than kiss her.

"Don't stop," she said, running her fingers through his long wavy hair, her breathing coming in short spurts.

And he didn't. He hadn't kissed a woman in a long time, not like this, maybe never like this, and it was as if a dam was breaking inside him, flooding him with feeling. The sensation of her hot, open mouth inviting him deeper and deeper inside her erased all the months of pain, all the self-doubt, all the darkness, and he reveled in it.

He slid his lips down the silky slope of her neck, beneath the curls of her golden hair. He kissed her in that sweet spot behind her ears, so redolent with her perfume, as she continued to bend against him, her arms winding around his strong, muscular torso, pulling him toward her, as if she couldn't get close enough to him, didn't want a single inch of air between them.

He kissed her throat and then the hollow just above her collarbone, letting his lips and tongue linger there in that glorious valley that belonged to her and only her.

"Oh, Ridge," she whispered, running her hands down his chest.

And then suddenly, as if someone had conspired to douse the flames of the sexual fire that had ignited between them at long last, Caroline's cell phone rang.

"It'll go to voicemail," she groaned. "Let it ring. I couldn't care less who it is."

"Not even if it's Ricky boy?" said Ridge, lifting his head up to try to see into her eyes.

"No, not even then." But it was she who pulled away, she who sat upright. "But oddly enough, this is a good time—the right time—for me to clarify the situation with Rick. I understand there's been a miscommunication."

"Not interested in hearing about the guy, honestly." But Ridge knew he had to hear about him; it *was* the right time, before they went any further. He'd let himself get carried away by the moment, by Caroline's infectious enthusiasm for life, by the way she made him feel, and he needed to get a grip, needed to face reality. Rick was a jerk, but he wasn't damaged, didn't need an attendant to take care of his daily needs, didn't spend hours in dimly lit rooms waiting for an array of numbing ointments to lessen the burning in his eyes. Yes, he needed to hear whatever she had to say.

"Rick and I haven't gotten back together, Ridge. Just so you know. It's important to me that you know."

"You spent the night with him, Caroline. He's planning your second honeymoon and he spoon-fed me the gory details, for God's sake. I may be blind but I'm not dumb."

"A second honeymoon? Are you joking?"

"Not in the slightest. He said he'd booked some swanky resort."

She shook her head. "There's no honeymoon because there's no wedding. And there's no wedding because he and I are not a couple again. We've had dinner a few times. Oh, and he did spend the night at my hotel suite with me—in the other room." She told him about the fog and some woman whose car was in an accident, who Rick hadn't been able to resist rescuing. "I'm glad he and I aren't estranged anymore, aren't fighting and hurling accusations at each other. But I guess he was trying to one-up you when he told you all that, the way you one-upped him when you took away his title at Forrester Creations, the way you two have been one-upping each other forever. I've been trying to stay out of it, like Switzerland."

"Switzerland hasn't always been neutral," he said with a smile. "They went to war in the nineteenth century. Maybe you should forget about food trucks, classical music and hockey and take a course in world history."

"Fine. Let's make that our next expand-Caroline's-horizons field trip." She hesitated, then said: "Besides, the old Ridge wouldn't have let Rick stand in his way if he really wanted something."

"Maybe not, but I'm not the old Ridge," he said, placing his sunglasses back over his eyes and securing them at the top of the bridge of his nose, signaling that the romantic portion of their excursion was over. The truth was he didn't care about Rick, what Rick wanted, what Rick thought he was entitled to. What Ridge cared about was Caroline and what was best for her—and it wasn't him.

I won't be a burden to any woman, least of all a woman like her, he vowed. *She's so vital, so young, with such a promising, full life ahead of her.* It would be selfish to deprive her of the happiness she deserves, and that happiness includes a man without physical limitations.

And yet, he wanted her. Of that there was no doubt.

Chapter Eleven

Despite his brief chill toward her at the end of their drive home from the Strip Crawl, Caroline was pleased that Ridge approached the final two weeks before the fundraiser with renewed gusto. It would have been difficult for him not to get caught up in the excitement. The scene at Forrester Creations was what she described as "controlled chaos," as harried employees from all departments worked overtime to ensure that no detail was left unattended. Everything had to be perfect for the big night when two hundred guests would fill the ballroom at Forrester Creations, be served an elegant dinner courtesy of Luc Bergeron and treated to an exclusive presentation showcasing Forrester Creations' spring collection. The guests had paid top dollar for tickets to the event, the profits from which would go toward cancer research in honor of Stephanie Forrester. The international media would be covering the fashion show in force and, with any luck, the company's luster and prestige would be on full display. A united front was essential, which meant that there could be no infighting between Ridge and Rick, especially not over her.

Toward that end, she agreed to attend the cocktail party that Hope had arranged at her mother's—Hope's way of thanking Caroline for her help with the designs. It was also Hope's intention, Caroline suspected, of doing a little matchmaking by bringing Rick and Caroline together in a family setting. She and Rick had both been so busy at work that there hadn't been as many romantic dinners alone together, only quick lunches between meetings. Caroline still cared about Rick—she couldn't just turn love on and off like a faucet—but the intensity wasn't there, and she knew it. She had invested her whole heart and soul in him when they were married and he had abused her devotion, shredded it, thrown it away on a night of mindless pleasure with Maya, and she couldn't summon up the energy to get the intensity back even if she'd wanted to—even if that intensity hadn't been transferred to Ridge.

Yes, she thought. *My feelings for Ridge Forrester, the man I'd once loathed, the man I'd viewed as a self-important bully who always got what he wanted no matter whom he hurt, are real and growing and passionate, and they aren't going away any time soon. He's changed and I've changed, and someday we ... Well, who knows what the future might bring?*

Though Ridge's vision was still bothersome, he wasn't letting it keep him from interacting with the rest of the team. He rode them hard, demanded answers to questions about every facet of the fundraiser; was a fully engaged CEO despite having to delegate the actual hands-on work. His face still lit up when Caroline walked into his office and he traded barbs with her over fabrics and models and her tendency to speak her mind, but there hadn't been any more after-hours field trips due to their crammed schedules. She missed their outings, missed her private moments with him outside the office, and she vowed that she would arrange at least one more before the big night, before she had to make a decision about whether to stay in LA or go home.

"Lovely as always," said Rick, appraising Caroline as they waited outside Brooke Logan's front door. "You dazzle me, you know that? Amazing dress."

Caroline laughed. "You've seen me in it before, Rick, but I'll happily take the compliment. Thank you."

He grabbed her hand and squeezed it. "I love you. Still. Always. Nothing's changed. Maybe you'll believe that after tonight."

"Why? What's happening tonight?" Caroline asked as she arched an eyebrow at him. "You're not planning another one of your surprises, are you?"

"So impatient, Ms Spencer." He grinned. "You'll just have to wait and see."

He's the handsomest man I've ever seen, Caroline thought for the hundredth time—*a Prince Charming straight from a fairy tale. There was nothing imperfect about his appearance, not the slightest flaw, not a feature out of proportion, and yet ...*

And yet it was Ridge's rugged face that floated constantly into her consciousness—from the craggy lines on his forehead and the slight bend at the bridge of his nose to the unruly beard and lumberjack hair. She giggled to herself about that beard; it had given her skin a bad case of beard burn after he'd kissed her in the limo. Her chin and cheeks had felt raw and inflamed the next morning, and she'd had to doctor the redness with makeup before going into the office, but it had been so worth it.

"Caroline! How nice to see you!" Brooke Logan swung open the door for them and promptly gave Caroline a hug. "I'm sorry I haven't been at the office to welcome you back, but I hope our little get-together will make up for it."

"Absolutely. Thanks for having me," said Caroline.

Brooke swept them into her house, aromatic with fresh flowers and scented candles. She was as beautiful as ever, a stunner with her long flaxen hair and vixen figure. Never one to shrink from her seductive appeal, she wore a geometric, black-and-white, silk-jersey wrap dress with a plunging neckline, a diamond pendant resting inside the folds of her cleavage. Caroline wondered how Ridge was able to resist her after all their years together, and she felt intimidated suddenly; maybe it was farcical to imagine that he could be attracted to her after having been with a goddess like Brooke. But then she reminded herself that he'd returned from Paris and ended their long relationship, announcing that he'd outgrown Brooke and their so-called destiny, that she was no longer the woman he needed, that she brought too much drama and turmoil to his life and that it was time for him to move on. Caroline wondered if Brooke would ever really move on. Though she seemed to be handling her coparenting of RJ reasonably well, she'd taken the breakup with Ridge hard. While she and Uncle Bill had shared a special bond and he'd campaigned aggressively to marry her, Brooke was directionless these days, searching for her purpose in life—not always a good place to be, as Caroline knew all too well.

Caroline and Rick greeted the others. Hope had brought along Caroline's cousin, Liam Spencer, and it was always good to see him. Those two star-crossed lovers had been engaged more times than Caroline could count and nobody knew if they'd ever get together and make it stick, but in the meantime they enjoyed each other's company. And off in the corner, fixing himself a scotch, was Uncle Bill, looking like this gathering was the last place on earth he wanted to be.

Caroline tiptoed up behind him and tapped him on the shoulder. He jumped and dropped an ice cube on his foot.

"Jeez. You scared me, kid."

Caroline laughed. "Nobody scares you, Uncle Bill."

"Good point. How's it going?" He nodded at Rick after taking a sip of his drink. "You two hitting it off? You know how I feel about the Forresters, but if you and Rick can get it together again, I'll force myself to show up at Eric's house for another wedding."

"You're incorrigible," said Caroline, shaking her head at her uncle. He was brash and in a hurry and expected people to have the same opinions as he did. Everything was clear to him—you were either in or out, yes or no, all or nothing—and it was always a task to explain to him that life was complicated and making decisions as important as the one he was telling her to make weren't easy. "I've been much too busy with the fundraiser to focus on my love life. You're coming, by the way, right? I know you're on the guest list."

He rolled his eyes. "I can't remember the last time I had to put on a monkey suit. Tuxes aren't my thing, but yeah, of course I'm coming. And Jarrett Maxwell, our crack reporter, will be covering the event for *Eye on Fashion*. Jarrett knows all and sees all, so you guys better be on your toes."

"I'm not worried. The rehearsals are going well and the designs are spectacular."

He smirked. "So you and the dressmaker have figured out how to get around his eyesight thing?"

Caroline groaned to herself. Her uncle loved coming up with putdowns for Ridge. He wrote him off as a prima donna and considered him unworthy both as a CEO and a romantic rival for Brooke, and he would explode at the mere thought of his niece swooning over him.

"Ridge and I had a bit of a bumpy start," Caroline said in a measured tone, "but we've worked together very well and we're both proud of what we've accomplished. He's really not the evil genius you make him out to be."

Bill scoffed. "Who said he was a genius? Your word, kid, not mine."

"You have a low opinion of him, I get it, Uncle Bill, but he *is* a genius when it comes to couture," said Caroline. "And he's well read and cultured and a huge sports fan, and if you took the time to get to know him, I think you'd—"

"Whoa! What do we have here?" He set his glass down on the coffee table and gave her a withering look. "You used to defend Rick with that kind of ferocity. Now you're singing the dressmaker's praises?"

"I'm just saying that some people are an acquired taste, Uncle Bill."

"Like rat poison is an acquired taste? Now be a good girl and go play with Rick." He spun her around and gave her a little shove.

The evening went smoothly, as everyone nibbled on hors d'oeuvres and chatted congenially, and while most of the conversation centered around Caroline, she fielded with good humor questions about how it felt to be back in LA, which design for the fashion show she was most excited about and which model would wear the show-stopper to close the show. Rick frequently wound his arm proprietarily around her waist and held her hand, acting as if they were a committed couple, and Caroline, not wanting to rock the boat, didn't make waves.

"What's new with RJ?" she asked Brooke at one point, sorry he wasn't home that evening.

"He's spending the night at Ridge's," said Brooke, her lips pursing with displeasure. "I do worry about the two of them alone in that big house. If something were to happen, Ridge wouldn't be able to do anything about it. The Stone Canyon Road area of Bel Air can be prone to wildfires, just like Malibu."

"But RJ's learned what to do in the event of a fire," Caroline said. "Ridge taught him all the dos and don'ts."

"And you know this how?" Rick asked her.

"Ridge told me," said Caroline. "He's very proud of his son and the way he takes his responsibilities seriously."

"Yes, well, that's all fine and good," said Brooke, "but the grown-up in that house isn't capable of taking charge in an emergency."

"That's not true," said Caroline. "Ridge manages very well and he can call Ben at a moment's notice if he needs help."

"Who the hell is Ben?" said Rick.

"He's a waiter at the Bel Air," Brooke said with a skeptical sigh. "As if that's a solution."

"I think it is," said Caroline, who explained about Ridge's arrangement with Ben with such specificity that they looked at her as if she'd sprouted three heads.

"What's any of this got to do with you?" asked Rick. "Have you met this guy?"

"Sure. I've been over there for work a few times," she said, realizing she'd again leaped to Ridge's defense without a second thought and her behavior had not gone unnoticed. "It gets crazy at the office with all the interruptions, so Ridge suggested I come to the house."

"Sounds like him," Rick said with a scowl. "He's all about making his loyal subjects bow down to him. Sounds cozy, too. All those dim lights, that moody music he likes, a little wine …"

Caroline felt her cheeks flush, both with the memory of Ridge's kisses in the limo and the anger at being backed into a corner by the man who'd betrayed her with another woman. "Do I look like anyone's 'loyal subject?'" she said more hotly than she meant to. "And I've been working hard for Forrester Creations since I came back, so it's logical that I'd go wherever and whenever I'm needed."

"Caroline's right, Rick," said Hope, rubbing her brother's shoulder to calm him down. "She and Ridge are business partners right now and you need to apologize for insinuating anything else."

Brooke laughed. "You really should apologize, honey," she scolded her son. "To think that anything could be going on between Ridge and Caroline is absurd."

Absurd, is it? Caroline thought, stung by Brooke's dismissal of her as a potential rival and irritated by Rick's relentless jealousy wherever Ridge was concerned.

"I'm sorry," said Rick, taking Caroline's hand and bringing it to his lips. "I love you, that's all." He glanced up at the others and his expression brightened. "Actually, I was planning to share our good news with everybody tonight."

Before Caroline could say "What good news?", Brooke and Hope squealed with delight.

"Is it what we're all hoping for?" Brooke asked, pressing her hands together.

Rick smiled. "Caroline has given me reason to believe I might have another shot at being her husband—not tomorrow or the next day, but someday soon." He reached into the pocket of his navy blue blazer and pulled out a small velvet box. He flipped it open and plucked out an exquisite ring. It was not the diamond-and-emerald beauty he'd given her with his last proposal, but an evening-sky blue sapphire surrounded by diamonds. He threaded it onto Caroline's finger, no bended knee this time but standing upright, shoulders squared, posture perfect. "In ancient customs, a gift of a sapphire was a pledge of trust and loyalty, which is what I pledge to you, Caroline, if you're willing."

As the others cooed with excitement over Rick's grand gesture, Caroline froze. She was overwhelmed, completely blindsided. A marriage proposal so quickly? After only a handful of dinners together? After having had no contact for six months while she was in New York? She knew he could be impulsive and she'd loved that about him once, but this—this surprise in front of his family was more than she could handle.

Still, with everyone regarding her expectantly, with Rick beseeching her with his eyes, Caroline needed to respond in a way that would be true to herself and fair to him. She needed to be honest, in other words, not about Ridge—this really was about her and Rick, no third party—and she wasn't sure how. What she *was* sure of in that moment was that she would never go back to him no matter how ardently he courted her, and she couldn't let him think otherwise. Stringing him along would be cruel and she wasn't that. Breaking the news to him in front of his mother and sister, however, would be a tricky business.

Don't just stand there like a mannequin. Think fast, Caroline, she urged herself. *Think of something diplomatic.*

"To say it's beautiful is an understatement, Rick." She gazed at the ring admiringly. The diamonds glistened and the sapphire was a shade of blue that was truly mesmerizing; he had good taste, no question about that. "And I'm incredibly flattered that you want us to begin again. We were a dynamite team the first time around and it was never boring being married to you, as your surprise tonight demonstrates." The others laughed affectionately. "But ..." She slid the ring off her finger and handed it back to the man who was no longer her one true love. "I'm going to let you hang onto it. It wouldn't be right for either of us to jump back into a relationship. Not now."

The room fell into a brief and awkward silence. Then a beaming Rick said, "See why I love this woman, everybody? She tells it like it is, no baloney. And hey, I'll take her answer any day. A 'not now' is a whole lot better than a 'never.'"

Except that she had implied a "never." She could have sworn she had. He just wasn't hearing it.

Chapter Twelve

"And here's my next appointment," said Eric, rising to greet Caroline as she breezed into the room.

"Don't get up," Caroline urged, bouncing onto the seat cushion next to him and planting a kiss on his cheek. "I thought you were supposed to be resting, not entertaining a parade of women."

"Always the spitfire," Eric said with a chuckle, clearly enjoying the implication.

"My cue to leave," said Pam, diving into her purse for her phone and in the process knocking Eric's reading glasses and legal pad off the coffee table. "Sorry. Very discombobulated today. If one more person texts me using the letters ASAP, I'll tear my hair out."

"Poor Pam," said Caroline, acknowledging how frazzled she must be, and with good reason.

Everybody at the office was moving at warp speed, trying to remember to dot every i and cross every t, but Pam was more highly strung than most. According to Donna, she was forgetting to relay phone messages and misplacing files—even letting her famously moist lemon bars go stale. "It'll all be over in a couple of days."

"Right." Pam tried to gather her belongings yet again only to have her own glasses slip out of her purse, along with a lipstick, and become wedged between the sofa cushions. "I'm going, I'm going," she said, finally retrieving her odds and ends.

When she was out the door, Eric sighed and took Caroline's hand. "Tell me. How are you?"

"Tired but invigorated too. I've loved every minute of the work here, Eric. Designing for the Forrester Creations couture line has been a privilege, and getting to show it off at the fundraiser will be that much more of a thrill."

"Then you were the right person for the job, and I'm so glad you agreed to take it," he said. "Now, about your other job, your less public one. My spies over there tell me my oldest son has been much more involved in Forrester Creations' business since you and I launched Project Ridge. From what I hear, he's not sitting alone in his office brooding, and it's all because of you and your nimble way of handling any assignment thrown at you. I asked you to come up with an idea for bringing back Ridge's spirit, his appetite for life, for the sake of the fundraiser and to silence all those buyers who've been skittish about the company's stability, and apparently you managed to do just that. Well done, Caroline."

"Truthfully, Eric, all I did was ask Ridge to help me expand my horizons." She laughed. "It sounds silly, I know, but he told me I should explore interests outside of the fashion industry, 'get out of the bubble,' as he calls it. So I came up with things I thought would be broadening for me—and not coincidentally appealing to him—and coaxed him into coming along for the ride. The idea was to drag him out of the house, pull him out of his sense of hopelessness, inspire him to embrace life again, and it worked. We went to a hockey game, the symphony, East LA for a sampling from all the food trucks ... There were some rocky moments, but overall he really seemed to enjoy it."

"Enjoy it? If I know my son at all, I bet he fell head over heels in love with you during all this expanding of your horizons."

Eric was clearly joking, but Caroline's heart banged in her chest. She asked herself if Eric could sense what had happened in the limo, how she and Ridge had kissed, how he'd said he'd been wanting to kiss her, how her body was still feeling the ripples of pleasure whenever she replayed those kisses in her mind. "What makes you say that?"

Eric smiled knowingly. "Why wouldn't he fall for you? Rick did. He told me he gave you an engagement ring, by the way."

"Yes, at Brooke's the other night, a beautiful ring. To say I was surprised is putting it mildly. He and I have mended fences over the past few weeks and I'm grateful for that, but it's just not going to happen for us this time. Too much baggage between us, I guess. I was planning to make it clear to him in case there was any misunderstanding—after the fundraiser. I don't want you to worry about the event for Stephanie, Eric. It'll be a display of Forrester family harmony. I'll make sure of it. I'll have a heart-to-heart talk with Rick after it's over and that'll be that. I'm sorry for both of us."

"He'll be sorry too." Eric narrowed his eyes at her. "But is the baggage between you the real reason it's not going to work out? Or maybe I wasn't so far off the mark when I made the crack about Ridge falling for you?" He cocked his head, his tone becoming serious. "Are my two sons about to do battle over you?"

She lowered her gaze, suddenly shy in front of the man who had been her father-in-law, the man who would be her father-in-law again if she and his oldest son ever—"Let's just say I've come to see an entirely different side of Ridge."

"Would you care to elaborate?"

Maybe it was Eric's kind, gentle tone or the fact that he'd always been so good to Caroline, or maybe it was that she missed her best friend Gigi and had no one else in whom she could truly confide, but either way she was ready to burst. "I—I think I'm in love with Ridge."

Eric inhaled deeply as he processed her news. "'Love' is a powerful word."

"I know, I know. It's crazy, right? He's older than I am. He was in love with Brooke forever and then with Katie. He's only been in my life on a daily basis for a couple of months. But if I'm really honest with myself, maybe there was something there even before I came back to LA. Why else would I have been walking around New York stewing over him, holding a grudge against him for taking away Rick's presidency? I spent way too much emotional energy on a man I supposedly hated. And then when I saw him at that party, out of the blue ..."

Eric looked baffled. "Maybe you should back up and start from the beginning."

Caroline took a deep breath and let her feelings come gushing forth. She admitted to Eric how much she'd resented Ridge after her divorce, blaming his humiliation of Rick for the affair with Maya. She told him how she ran into him at Luc's opening and then how she'd stood up to him that first day back in his office after he'd criticized every word out of her mouth. She recounted how well they'd collaborated on his designs, how he'd asked about her life, her goals, her interests; how he'd prodded her to seek new experiences, how they'd shared some of those experiences together; how they'd kissed, how Ridge had said he'd been longing to kiss her. Yes, she even told him that.

He listened with rapt attention to all of it without passing judgment—without saying a word, in fact—and it was only at the end of her narrative, after she stopped to collect her thoughts, that he said simply, "You do realize this could get complicated."

"Maybe," she acknowledged. "And maybe not. I could be delusional about Ridge's interest in me, which would make my interest in him a moot point and Rick would never need to know about it."

"That's not what I meant by complicated, although I do worry about stirring up my sons' already overheated rivalry." Eric sighed, his brows furrowed with concern. "I was actually thinking about Ridge's eyesight. The specialist on the case believes the blindness will recede completely, but in the meantime are you prepared to have a life with a man who'll be depending on you for even the most basic tasks? You're a tough, capable young woman, but it's one thing to collaborate on fashion designs and quite another to be the caretaker for the one you love. I know. I've been there."

"I don't run away from challenges, even one with that kind of responsibility," Caroline said, straightening her posture to emphasize the strength of her convictions. "I've never told anyone at Forrester Creations about this, not even Rick, but as part of my work with my foundation on behalf of cancer research, I met a man I became very close to. His name was Terry Jarvis and he was the head of marketing for one of the big record companies. I fell in love with him, Eric. He was handsome and smart and funny, and he had brain cancer. And because his tumor was located in the occipital lobe, he lost his sight after we met. Did his blindness stop me from caring about him? Did I care about him because I felt sorry for him? Did I ever once think of him as a burden, even though he was no longer the hot guy who swept me off my feet? No, no and no. Ridge is hardly dying of a terminal illness, so the only comparison I'm making between him and Terry is that if I say I'm ready to be his eyes, be his light, I mean it. I've done it."

"I'm sorry for your loss, of course, and I appreciate your sharing something so personal with me, but sometimes it's not up to us," he said, gazing at Stephanie's portrait. "Sometimes they don't want us to make sacrifices for them. It's possible that Ridge takes after his mother in that respect. He's a proud man. He may not want to be your 'challenge,' Caroline."

"Then I'll just have to convince him otherwise," she said resolutely.

*

"I thought we were going dancing," said Caroline when she arrived at Ridge's house that evening and found him upstairs in his bedroom napping instead of waiting by the front door for her limo. It was their last opportunity for another field trip before the fundraiser, and she'd gotten them tickets to a Hollywood Hills blues club with a band and a dance floor.

"Could we have a raincheck?" he asked, his voice husky with the vestiges of a sound sleep, his hair askew across the pillows of his king-sized bed. He was wearing blue jeans with holes at the knees and a yellow T-shirt emblazoned with the logo of RJ's soccer team, and he looked like a little boy, albeit it one with a beard. "Must be all the pre-fundraiser stuff at the office. Just knocked me out."

"Is it your eyes?" Caroline asked gently from the threshold. "Are you in pain, Ridge?"

"No more than usual, no," he said. "Just beat."

Caroline stepped further into the bedroom, its lights dimmed, its drapes drawn, and took a peek at her surroundings. She'd never been granted entry before and it was the essence of Ridge Forrester: rugged and masculine. The color palette was gray, black and white—muted and modern—and there was a fireplace off in a cozy corner and an animal print rug on the hardwood floor. Beyond was a sumptuous master bathroom as large as most people's living rooms, also in shades of gray, black and white.

He could use a woman's touch, Caroline thought with smile. *Nothing too frou-frou, but some flowers here and there, a cashmere throw and maybe some pink. Yes, definitely some pink.*

"Well," she said cheerfully. "If you aren't up to the dancing, then the dancing will have to come to you."

She searched the room for his audio equipment, knowing he'd have the latest electronic gear. Inside a built-in cabinet that matched the bed's headboard, she found an iPod dock and his music library and then located his speakers. Perfect.

As she scrolled through the songs, she hit on several classic blues tunes but realized she didn't want Ridge to have to listen to lyrics about heartbreak and choruses of "My baby left me." Not tonight. Tonight was about her and Ridge, about exploring *their* horizon as a couple, and heartbreak was the last thing on her mind.

"I think we should skip the blues and go for some rock 'n' roll," she said as she continued to scour his library. "We should liven up this place."

"I'm not feeling lively," said Ridge, "but if I take a quick shower I'll probably snap out of my fog. Do you mind?"

"No problem," she said. "Should I ask if you need help with anything or will you bite my head off?"

He smiled. "I can find my way to the shower, Caro. I can even brush my own teeth. And if I really, really try, I can use the toilet all by my little self."

She raised her hands in surrender. "Okay, okay. I'll stop."

"Actually, I do need your help. I'll want a change of clothes." He directed her to his closet and asked her to pick out a pair of jeans, a white T-shirt and a fresh pair of briefs.

Caroline completed her tasks and handed the clothes to Ridge, reminded of Eric's words about how proud he was and how resistant he was to appearing needy. And yet he'd asked for her help and she'd provided it. They *could* do this. They could do it *together*.

Ridge walked slowly into the bathroom, bracing himself for any stray objects in his path, and closed the door. While he was gone, Caroline sat in one of the two chairs by the fireplace.

I'm right where I want to be, she thought, as she listened to the water running in the shower, *right here with the man who makes me feel needed, alive, the best person I can be.*

At one point Ridge started humming and his voice echoed against the tiles. It was a tune she couldn't identify because he didn't so much hum as croak in his raspy voice, but it made her smile because it reinforced how far he'd come from the morose man who'd barked at her on her first day back.

Yes, she was happy just to be in that room waiting for him. She'd spent so much time in New York rushing to this party and that gala, playing the social butterfly with acquaintances who didn't care about her anymore than she cared about them, never touching down for very long for fear of being bored, of being alone, of being unloved. She didn't know if Ridge Forrester loved her, but she knew he was opening up to the possibility, and it sent her spirits soaring.

She heard the water shut off and more humming, and then he appeared in the open bathroom door.

"I've made a momentous decision," he said, looking wide awake in the fresh clothes she'd chosen for him. "And I'd really like your input."

Caroline rose from the chair. "Of course."

"Come here."

"In the bathroom?"

"That's what this is, Caro: a bathroom. I've decided it's time to shave off my beard and you're going to do the deed, along with giving my hair a trim. I should look my Forrester best for the fundraiser, shouldn't I?"

Caroline gulped. It was one thing to be his caregiver, but take a razor to his face? In a room with all the lights dimmed? She was strong willed but not a magician. "You want me to shave you?"

He laughed. "And I thought Caroline Spencer was fearless. You're terrified. Admit it."

He was right: she was terrified. But admit it? Not a chance. "I'm totally fine with it."

"Sure you are. If it'll ease your mind at all, I'll be turning up the lights in here once I put on my glasses. And I'll walk you through it all, so you won't have to pretend you have your barber's license."

Caroline swallowed the giant lump of anxiety in her throat and joined Ridge in the cavernous master bathroom, where he'd set up a chair in front of the mirror. He put on his dark glasses, turned up the lights as he'd promised, told her where she'd find the razor, the shaving cream, the scissors and the towels and gave her step-by-step instructions in the art of shaving.

"The first thing with this much growth is to take the scissors and cut the beard as close to the skin as possible—without killing me," he said as he sat in the chair, a large white towel draped over his chest. "You have to clip it piece by piece until it's basically just short stubble."

"Right," she said and started clipping, letting the hairs fall onto the towel. When she was a little girl, she used to cut pretty dresses out of magazines and collect them in a journal—that was the sum total of her experience with scissors. But she was trying to stay calm in order to prepare herself for the much scarier job: using the razor.

"You're awfully quiet—for you," he said after she'd been working on the beard for fifteen minutes.

"I'm just taking it slowly," she said. "But I'm done now and ready for step two. The razor, right?"

"Cock a doodle doo!" He lifted his elbows like a squawking rooster.

Caroline laughed. "I'm not a chicken, so be quiet."

"Actually, you're very brave. Step two is the shaving cream, not the razor. Whip it into a nice, thick, foamy lather, then use the brush to apply it over the stubble."

Caroline did as she was told and discovered that if she imagined his face as a dessert and she was covering it in whipped cream, her hands wouldn't shake. She slathered the shaving cream over him artfully, making sure she didn't miss any spots, and then she gave him a second coat.

"You look like Santa Claus," she giggled as she took a minute to view her handiwork.

"No stalling, Caro. Get on with it."

Caroline reached for the shiny, chrome-plated razor on the counter and reminded herself that razors were not necessarily weapons of destruction.

She ran the razor over his left cheek in a slow, downward motion, just under his sideburn as he'd instructed her. And then she continued over the rest of his face, slowly, carefully, telling herself the worst that could happen was that she'd nick his skin in a thousand places and he'd start bleeding profusely and she'd have to call Ben for help and—*No, stop it, Caroline.*

"You're not bad at this," Ridge mumbled, trying not to move his mouth.

"Shush. I'm getting to the mustache next."

She was deliberate in her strokes and gaining confidence with each one, and before she knew it, she'd tackled his entire face without so much as a scratch.

"There." She stood back and admired his clean-shaven reflection in the mirror. "All done."

"God, you're good. When I do it myself, I end up with at least a nick or two."

"As you said, Ridge, I'm good."

They both laughed.

"Ready for the next step?" he asked.

"I am."

She grabbed a moist face towel and wiped away the remnants of the shaving cream, then patted his skin with a dry towel. "And now the cologne?"

"The aftershave," he corrected her. "The bottle should be right there with the other tools of the trade. Pour just a little bit in the palm of your hand and then splash it—gently—on my baby-soft skin."

She found the bottle, opened the cap and smelled it. It was a spicy-sweet scent that, according to the label, contained shea butter, aloe, chamomile and green tea. Then she dribbled a handful of the lotion into her palm and patted his face with it.

"One more step and we're finished," he said. "My hair. Can't do a thing with it."

"Piece of cake." Caroline trimmed the ends and evened them out, and by the time she put down the scissors he was the old Ridge, the one she'd run into in New York—with one big difference: she was in love with this Ridge and she prayed he felt the same way.

"From what I can make out in the mirror, I don't look half bad," he said, cocking his head at his reflection, "although it's like staring at a picture in a frame that's been cracked in a dozen places."

"You look movie-star handsome, Ridge," she said, hoping to keep his mood buoyant, knowing how impossibly difficult his condition had been for him. "You really do. Now lean back while I finish the job."

She began to massage his head and scalp with her fingers.

"I bet you'd get nice money for this," he said, his voice husky and low. "You have the touch." He turned toward her and felt for her hands and held them. "Thank you. Seriously, thank you. Now, how about taking me for a road test?"

"You want to go out?" said Caroline. "I thought you were exhausted."

"I meant road test my clean-shaven face, right here, right now. I'm not the least bit tired. Don't you know what a turn-on that was? Having you shave me like that? I told you that a full life is about using all the senses, and mine are on fire right now—in the best way possible."

He stood up, wrapped his arms around her waist and drew her close to him, so close her breasts were crushed against his chest, her belly pressed against his hardness, and she could feel herself growing moist. And then he kissed her, devouring her lips with such intensity that she had to take a break to catch her breath.

"Come with me," he murmured. "Be with me." He clasped her hand and she led him back into the bedroom where he sat her on the bed and removed his glasses, setting them on the night table. "I wouldn't trust just anybody to do what you did in there, Caro. But I trust you. Let me show you how much."

"I may die if you don't." Caroline's pulse raced as he brought his lips down on hers again. Her whole body sprang to life as it occurred to her that there was no limo driver to inhibit them this time, no back seat to constrict them, no member of the Forrester Creations team to demand their attention. They were alone together and they wanted each other and it was happening—very fast but not fast enough to keep pace with her desire.

"Ridge," she purred, although it was more of a sigh of longing. He ran his hands over her, anywhere, everywhere. He unbuttoned her blouse and unhooked her bra, not with the fumbling of a blind man but with the deftness of a craftsman, with the hands of the artist he was. He traced the outline of her breasts with his fingertips and circled her erect nipples as if he were sketching her bare flesh. He was creating an indelible image of the curves and arcs of her body, both for himself, to compensate for not being able to see her clearly, and for her gratification. And when he lowered his head to take each breast into his mouth, to suck on them, flick his tongue over them, she cried out with the moan of a woman she'd never known she could be, a woman whose entire being was ablaze with passion, a woman who was anticipating the exquisite sensation of him touching her in the place that was throbbing with dampness and desire. Yes, it was all happening very fast and she was ready. She'd been waiting for a man like Ridge Forrester her entire life.

"How I wish I could see you without limitations," he whispered, finding the zipper of her skirt and tugging it downward, allowing him to reach inside her lacy panties, slip his graceful fingers into her moist heat and stroke her there.

"You more than see me," she gasped as she arched into him, her brain scrambled with the electric currents convulsing through her body. She wriggled out of her skirt and panties as quickly as she could, so desperate was she to shed every barrier between them. "You see inside me. I want to see inside you too."

Needing no further encouragement, Ridge yanked off his T-shirt and unzipped his jeans, then stood for just a moment so he could free himself of all his clothes, and then brought his nakedness, his hardness and his hungry mouth down on her.

"Caro," he murmured, the word shooting vibrations through both of them. "Caro. I knew it would be like this ... So good, so right ..."

Caroline's insides turned to mush as he whispered to her, as he encouraged her, as he punctuated his words with penetrating kisses. She wrapped her quivering thighs around his waist, grabbed his back, splaying her fingers against his skin and gasping as he thrust himself into her, then drew out, then in again and out. He rotated his tight, muscular hips not with ferocity but rather with a craving, a yearning, establishing a rhythm that synced blissfully with hers.

"So good, so right," she repeated, clutching his perfectly chiseled buttocks and urging him deeper and deeper into her, so deep he filled her completely and caused her to rear up and meet his face, look him straight in his wounded eyes. "Never expected to feel like this."

He thrust inside her again, his body slick with the commingling of her arousal and his. "I want us to feel it together, go there together. Hang on, Caro." He moved in and out as she clung to his waist, his back, his face, any place she could touch.

"Don't stop," she moaned, the muscles inside her contracting, the wave beginning to rise up and swallow her as he loomed over her, each thrust sweeping the wave closer to the shore. "I'm ... Oh God, Ridge."

The wave crested with his final thrust and he cried out along with her, "Yes ... Yes ... Caro ..." He shuddered, his body smashing into hers one more time, their every fiber and membrane pulsating with their climax.

Her eyelids fluttered as he rolled off her slowly and then cradled her in his arms. "Did that just happen?" she said, her body still palpitating with the force of their love.

"Yeah, and it needs to happen again." He kissed her. "Sooner rather than later."

"Sooner rather than later," she repeated with a contented sigh. "After I catch my breath and—"

A knocking at the front door, a *pounding*, as with a fist, interrupted her. *Thump! Thump! Thump!*

"Are you kidding me?" said Ridge.

"At least whoever it is waited until the 'Oh Gods' were over," said Caroline, and they both laughed.

But the pounding started again and they untangled from each other, startled and exasperated by the abrupt intrusion.

Caroline sighed, remembering when her cell phone rang while they'd kissed in the limo. "Foiled again."

"Can't imagine who'd be coming over at this time of night," Ridge grumbled, begrudgingly putting his glasses back on, along with his clothes, "and why they aren't using the doorbell."

"Could it be RJ?"

"He's got a key. But I guess it could be Brooke with something important about RJ—or something she thinks is important. In any case, to be continued." He leaned down and kissed Caroline on the mouth, a hot soulful kiss meant to endure long after his lips left hers. And then he stood back up and walked toward the bedroom door.

"Wait. I'm not letting you go alone," said Caroline, hurrying into her own clothes so she was presentable. Then she hooked her arm through his and together they descended the stairs, the persistent pounding on the door reverberating throughout the house.

"Hold on. I'm coming," Ridge muttered as they descended the staircase.

When they reached the foyer, it was Caroline who spotted the figure in the window panels that framed the front door—not Brooke at all but a male figure ... a figure that was shifting from one foot to the other as if impatient to be granted entry to the house ... a figure she recognized instantly.

Chapter Thirteen

"Rick, what a surprise," Caroline said, taking a quick mental inventory of her appearance. Was her blouse unbuttoned? Her skirt unzipped? Her lipstick smeared? She couldn't very well dash into the powder room to check.

"To what do I owe this visit?" Ridge said, not bothering to hide his disdain. "Business, emergency or social call?"

Rick strutted past Ridge and Caroline into the living room, an oddly self-satisfied smirk on his face, and planted himself in the middle of the room, his arms folded across his chest, defiant. "Both," he said. "I thought I'd drop in to see how Project Ridge is coming along."

"No idea what you're talking about, Ricky, and don't really care," said Ridge. "It's late. Big fundraiser coming up in a couple of days, in case you haven't been paying attention. Just say whatever it is that's got you so unhinged and go home."

"Is that what you want me to do, Caroline?" Rick glared at her as if accusing her of something. "Should I tell him what you and my father have been up to? Or would that put a monkey wrench in the *Forrester family harmony* you were so determined to stage for the fundraiser?"

Ridge turned to Caroline. "What's his problem this time? Or is it just the usual Daddy-loves-me-more hostility?"

"Rick," said Caroline, trying to stay calm but growing bored with his antics. "I'm not 'up to' anything." He could be a hothead, especially when it involved Ridge—the morning he'd answered her cell phone in her hotel suite while she was in the shower was recent evidence of that. But whatever current grudge brought him to the house that night was a mystery.

He laughed mirthlessly. "You tell me. You've been playing Ridge for weeks now. Have you gotten him into bed yet? Is that what I walked in on? And was it worth it, just to keep the couture buyers happy and rack up more orders for Forrester Creations? Are you that ambitious? Would you sink that low?"

"You're drunk," Caroline snapped, smelling alcohol on his breath. "But that's no excuse for talking to me like that." She had to restrain herself from whipping her hand across his face for what he was implying. How dare he cast her as the promiscuous one after what he'd done with Maya. "You're upset that I'm here with Ridge instead of out with you. But I've told you more than once that we work at his house sometimes. We accomplish a lot when there are no interruptions."

"What's this about the buyers? If this is about the fundraiser, I wish you'd tell me what's going on. I'm not interested in last-minutes glitches, not after all the months of planning and hard work."

"Hey, don't worry about a thing," said Rick. "Your little friend here has you covered. Your dresses will be fine and all the ladies will write big checks to honor Stephanie's memory."

"Then what is it?" Ridge demanded, his voice rising.

"This." Rick reached into his jacket pocket, pulled out a small black device and waved it in the air. "It's all right here."

Ridge turned to Caroline again, exasperated. She knew he couldn't see the device clearly enough to make out what it could be.

"It's one of those digital recorders," she said with a shrug, in the dark just as Ridge was.

"It's Pam's," said Rick. "She left it at Dad's this morning. She was recording his speech for the fundraiser and must have forgotten it when Caroline showed up. My former wife makes a lot of house calls, it seems. She was Dad's next meeting."

"So what?" Ridge challenged.

"Eric wanted a status update on the fashion show," Caroline explained to him. "I was happy to give him one."

"Makes sense," said Ridge. "What the hell does a tape recorder have to do with me or Caroline, Rick? Just go home and sleep it off, would you, please?"

Rick patted the recorder as if it were an unearthed treasure chest that contained the clue to some long-hidden truth. "Dad found this under the couch not long after Caroline left. I stopped by a little later and he asked me to return it to Pam at the office tomorrow morning. I decided to play it back first, so I could hear what he plans to say at the shindig, and, man, did I get an earful. Hot stuff on that recorder."

"For the love of God," Ridge said wearily. "Spit it out already."

"Pam must have forgotten to hit stop," said Rick. "She can be a little scatterbrained, your aunt Pam. So her recorder kept recording even after she left—until the battery ran out, that is. Anyway, it recorded Dad's speech, but it also recorded something more, which turned out to be a really juicy conversation between Dad and Caroline. I decided to do you a favor, Ridge, and let you listen to it. It's muffled but plenty audible."

Caroline felt her stomach lurch. What, specifically, had she and Eric been discussing that Rick would qualify as "juicy"? He was clearly hoping to use the recorder to incriminate her or to embarrass Ridge or to pay them both back for some perceived slight, but how?

"May I do the honors?" Rick asked, but the question was rhetorical. He had every intention of pressing play himself. "Fasten your seatbelts, everybody."

Caroline swallowed hard as she prepared herself for Rick's stunt, whatever it might be, even as she racked her brain, trying to anticipate what mischief, what hurt, he was about to inflict. She'd loved him once, loved him unconditionally, in spite of his jealousies and insecurities. But now she feared that he was capable of acting in a way that would destroy any remaining affection she had for him—and, worse, that he was about to burst the bubble of perfect happiness she'd shared with Ridge only minutes before.

"Tell me. How are you?"

"Tired but invigorated too. I've loved every minute of the work here, Eric. Designing for the Forrester Creations couture line has been a privilege, and getting to show it off at the fundraiser will be that much more of a thrill."

"Then you were the right person for the job, and I'm so glad you agreed to take it."

It was Eric's voice. Caroline's too. She remembered he'd asked her about the fashion show, about whether they were on track. A harmless enough conversation, she thought with relief.

"Now, about your other job, your less public one. My spies over there tell me my oldest son has been much more involved in Forrester Creations' business since you and I launched Project Ridge. From what I hear, he's not sitting alone in his office brooding, and it's all because of you and your nimble way of handling any assignment thrown at you. I'd asked you to come up with an idea for bringing back Ridge's spirit, his appetite for life, for the sake of the fundraiser and to silence all those buyers who've been skittish about the company's stability, and apparently you managed to do just that. Well done, Caroline."

Ridge looked stung by his father's words, his back stiffening even as his shoulders sagged. "So there really is a 'Project Ridge?'" he asked her.

"It was just a phrase Eric used, an innocent label for my collaboration with you on the designs," she said offhandedly, hoping to dispel any notion Ridge might have that she and Eric were plotting against him. They were only trying to help him by distracting him from his dark thoughts. At least *she* was. "You know how frustrated your father has been, not being able to pitch in at the company, not being around to design with you. He's having a tough time letting go, that's all."

"And since when have the buyers been skittish about Forrester Creations?" he said defensively. "Have they been telling Dad they've lost faith in me? Have they been whispering in his ear about the CEO who was brilliant when he was the hero who rescued his son in the fire but isn't so brilliant when he can't read the numbers on profit and loss reports?"

"Ridge, I have no idea about the buyers or what they think," said Caroline. "I have no idea who Eric talks to or why, either."

"Obviously he talks to *you*," Ridge growled. "What was that about bringing back 'my appetite for life?'"

"Allow the recorder to answer that," said a grinning Rick, deriving satisfaction from the increasing tension in the room.

"Truthfully, Eric, all I did was ask Ridge to help me expand my horizons. It sounds silly, I know, but he told me I should explore interests outside of the fashion industry, 'get out of the bubble,' as he calls it. So I came up with things I thought would be broadening for me—and not coincidentally appealing to him—and coaxed him into coming along for the ride. The idea was to drag him out of the house, pull him out of his sense of hopelessness, inspire him to embrace life again, and it worked. We went to a hockey game, the symphony, East LA for a sampling from all the food trucks ... There were some rocky moments, but overall he really seemed to enjoy it."

Caroline couldn't see Ridge's eyes behind the sunglasses, but she couldn't miss the expression on his face. His mouth, the same mouth that had caressed her so hungrily, formed a tight, straight line and his chin, the same chin she'd had such a challenge shaving because of his dimple, jutted out, his jaw set. "You told my father about all that?" he said to her, his tone both disbelieving and indignant. "I thought what we did was personal, something just between you and me. And yet you're discussing me with him, as if I were some sort of rat in a lab experiment—sorry, a rat in a lab *project*. And then there's the fact that you chose outings that were *my* interests, not yours. Hockey? Classical music? Tacos? You couldn't care less about any of that." He moved to a chair and sank down in it, deflated. "Quite a trap you set, Caroline, and I stumbled right into it. But then what did you expect from a blind man? That's what you thought, right?"

"It wasn't a trap at all," she protested. "I did want to learn about sports and classical music and ethnic foods, and you were the perfect person to mentor me. Oh, Ridge. Eric was just worried about you. He's your father and he loves you, and he didn't know how to talk to you; you weren't very approachable, if you remember. When I got to LA and saw how you were struggling, I was only too glad to do whatever he asked if it would help you and Forrester Creations. Yes, I wanted to lift your spirits, and in doing so, you lifted mine when you agreed to go with me on these outings.

I wasn't feeling very confident when I came back here and I have Rick to thank for that"—she gave him a sarcastic salute—"but you made me feel useful again, as if I could do anything."

"And you did," Ridge said scornfully. "Anything and everything my father asked you to—behind my back. You were very useful."

"Hang on, you two," said Rick, nodding at the recorder, which he had put on pause so Caroline and Ridge could argue. "You're missing the best part." He hit play.

"Enjoy it? If I know my son at all, I bet he fell head over heels in love with you during all this expanding of your horizons."

"What makes you say that?"

"Why wouldn't he fall for you? Rick did. He told me he gave you an engagement ring, by the way."

"Yes, at Brooke's the other night, a beautiful ring. To say I was surprised is putting it mildly. He and I have mended fences over the past few weeks and I'm grateful for that, but it's just not going to happen for us this time. Too much baggage between us, I guess. I was planning to make it clear to him in case there was any misunderstanding—after the fundraiser. I don't want you to worry about the event for Stephanie, Eric. It'll be a display of Forrester family harmony. I'll make sure of it. I'll have a heart-to-heart talk with Rick after it's over and that'll be that. I'm—"

"Aw, sorry, folks," said Rick after the recorder shut off abruptly. "The battery must have run out at that point, so we won't get to hear the rest. But you guys probably have enough to chew on."

As Rick tucked the recorder back in his jacket pocket, Ridge barked at him to get out and Caroline could only nod her assent. She couldn't wait to have Ridge to herself, to sit down with him and explain what came after the recorder stopped, when she'd poured out her heart to Eric about how she'd fallen in love with him. He needed to hear that part, needed to know with absolute certainty that what had happened upstairs between them, their lovemaking, their passion, their outpouring of feelings for each other, weren't the result of any premeditated plan or scheme or *trap*.

"Bottom line is I saved you the trouble of having that 'heart-to-heart' talk with me, Caroline," said Rick as he headed to the front door. "I got the message loud and clear. No repeat walk down the aisle for us? Understood. I won't pretend I'm not pissed off and disappointed, but it does soften the blow to know you won't be hooking up with this guy." He sneered at Ridge. "Not anymore. 'Night, you two."

There was an eerie silence in the house after Rick's car noisily peeled out of the driveway. Caroline started to speak, but Ridge's body language inhibited her. He'd gotten up, walked slowly out of the living room into the library and positioned himself behind his desk, his fort. He sat there motionless, in total darkness save for the light of the nearly full moon, while she stood there watching him, aching for him.

Eventually, she rallied herself, pulled up a chair and sat beside him. She was weak from all the drama, her legs as wobbly, but she was dying to touch him, to stroke his cheek at least, to reestablish their connection, soothe his hurt feelings, but she sensed that any attempt at physical contact would be extremely unwelcome. Still, it was time to plunge in, make him understand. She cleared her throat.

"Ridge, I—"

"Don't even think about saying, 'I can explain.'"

"Fine," she said. "How's this then: I love you."

Caroline let her declaration hang in the air for several seconds, her heart thumping in her chest with each and every ticking of the antique clock on the wall. When there was virtually no response from him, not even a flicker of recognition, she pressed on. "That's what's missing from the conversation on the recorder, Ridge. I told Eric I'd fallen in love with you. I don't know exactly when my feelings for you turned into love—maybe it was all the way back in New York when I ran into you at Luc's opening—but I went from thinking you were a judgmental, self-important tyrant to dreaming about the future we could have together, the future we *will* have together, because you love me too. I know you do."

He'd removed his glasses by this time and when he looked at her, it wasn't with love. "Don't flatter yourself," he said coldly. "I don't love easily or often, contrary to popular belief. And I sure as hell don't love if I don't trust."

"Wasn't that you who trusted me to shave your baby-soft face tonight?" Caroline lightened her tone, hoping he'd flash back to how playful it had been between them in his bathroom, how natural and easy, how right.

"Honey, I wouldn't trust you to tie the laces on my shoes."

"Ridge." She sighed. "Fine, so it sounded to you as if Eric and I were tricking you somehow. We weren't. Rick blew this whole thing out of proportion."

"Rick's an ass, but it wasn't *his* voice on that recorder."

"I'm just saying that Eric was concerned about you. As for me, well, that day in your office when you asked me what I wanted out of life, what my goals were, my interests outside of fashion … No one had ever asked me those questions and I began to look at you in a whole new way. You were so generous and kind to ask me about myself. I thought that if I spent time with you outside the office exploring the interests we talked about, it might be beneficial for both of us. Is that so unforgivable?"

"What's unforgivable is that you and Dad view me as someone to be pitied."

"What?" Caroline bolted out of the chair, flung her arms around Ridge's shoulders and buried her head in the curve of his neck. "You couldn't be more wrong. You're a strong, gifted, ridiculously attractive man who owns me, body and soul. The last thing I feel for you is pity."

Ridge shook his head. "You left out blind on that list of adjectives."

Caroline picked up her head so she could look into his face, look deeply into his eyes, the eyes that caused him so much pain. Still holding onto his shoulders as if to make sure he didn't run off, she said, "If you'd been able to listen to the rest of the recording, you would have heard Eric ask me if I could handle it if your sight didn't come back. I didn't hesitate, Ridge. I said yes unequivocally and I explained how I knew I could handle it. I love you. I don't think of you as impaired or defective or any less of a man. I happen to believe your sight will come back, but even if it doesn't, I'm here for the long haul and I told Eric that. He'll confirm it."

"Sure he will. He's your partner in crime. But the proof isn't on the recorder, as you point out, so we'll never really know. Stupid batteries, huh?"

Caroline heaved a defeated sigh, removed her hands from his shoulders and stood before him. "Please don't do this. Don't shut down on me again."

*

Shut down on her? If she only knew, Ridge
thought with a heavy heart. He yearned to pick
her up in his arms and carry her back upstairs and
make love to her over and over until dawn. All
he wanted was her, every waking moment of the
day and night and in his dreams too. She'd done
precisely what she'd set out to do and brought
back his appetite for life, and he was more than
grateful. He was in love with her, crazy in love
with her. *That* was the insurmountable problem,
not what she and his father did or said. Once he
got past the fact that it was Rick who had brought
the recorder to the house like a dog with a bone,
Rick who had been trying to stick it to him as he
always did, Ridge realized that she and his father
were only trying to help him and the company,
and their motives were pure.

No, the problem wasn't that she wanted to
help him. The problem was that she thought he
needed help. He did love her and he believed she
loved him too, but there was no getting around
the reality that he was blind. Not completely blind
anymore, but blind enough to destroy a relationship. He'd never been the one who needed
rescuing and the idea was utterly foreign to him,
repellent to him. He was the one his family looked
to for rescuing, not the other way around. He'd
rescued RJ, hadn't he? That was his role. He was

Ridge Forrester, the guy everybody could depend on, lean on, the guy they called in a crisis. Now? Now he was the guy who needed a waiter from the Bel Air Hotel to come to the house and make him a sandwich.

I vowed I'd never be a burden to her, Ridge reminded himself even as he was sorely tempted to tell his beautiful, smart, funny Caro how he really felt about her, how much he loved her. He couldn't. She was young and vivacious, the girl who enjoyed dressing up and going to parties and having fun. She didn't know the first thing about taking care of a broken man, let alone one with sight loss, and why should she? No, she deserved someone who embraced life as ferociously as she did. He was no longer the hero who could rescue her from a wildfire, but he could still be the man who stepped aside because it was best for her. He would not be her burden. And the sooner he cut the cord the better.

"I think you should leave, Caroline."

"You're tired," she said, nodding. "It's been a long day, so get some sleep. We've got the rehearsal tomorrow morning. I'll be overseeing the models while they're trying on the—"

"No, I mean leave LA," he interrupted, not wanting to prolong the explanation or the agony of the goodbye. "Thomas can take over your work on the fashion show from here on. Your services at Forrester Creations are no longer required. I'll make the jet available as soon as it's convenient for you to pack your things and check out of your hotel."

Caroline's jaw dropped. "Are you firing me, Ridge?"

"I'm letting you go," he said, his words weighted with the double meaning only he could understand.

She stood there openmouthed, eyes glistening. She wiped away the tears as they slipped down her cheeks and tossed her hair back off her shoulders. She reached for her purse on the chair, pulled out her phone and texted her limo driver to pick her up.

"Memo to you, Ridge," she said crisply after the driver texted back that he was already outside waiting for her. "I finish what I start. So yes, I'll go back to New York, but not until the fundraiser's over. I'll leave right after the last model walks down the runway. Is that soon enough for you?"

Ridge nodded, unable to speak for fear of letting her hear the catch in his voice.

"Just one thing before I go," she said, edging slowly out of the room, out of his house, out of his whole world. "You're the one who's constantly telling me that the key to enjoying life to the fullest is using all our senses, right?"

Ridge didn't answer, couldn't answer. So he let her speak, knowing she wouldn't leave without stating her opinion in no uncertain terms, the way she always did.

"You used your sense of taste when we took the trip to East LA and stopped at every food truck; your sense of smell too," she went on. "You used your sense of hearing when we went to the symphony. You used your sense of touch when we made love upstairs." She didn't bother to hide the single tear that escaped. "Since you're so literary and well read, you must have heard the proverb, 'There are none so blind as those who will not see.' It applies here, Ridge. You keep talking about being pitied. But if you ask me, the only person who pities you is you."

She turned on her heel and walked out.

Chapter Fourteen

Caroline used to live for fashion shows at Forrester Creations. While others in the industry often wilted under the myriad of details involved in putting on a flawless show or suffered acute anxiety at the thought of all the fashionistas, retail buyers and unforgiving media scrutinizing their designs, she adored the high-octane, adrenaline-charged atmosphere and she had a knack for remaining cool, calm and thoroughly in command.

The fashion show for the fundraiser to honor Stephanie Forrester and raise money for cancer research was no different. Despite the fact that she hadn't slept or eaten, that her body felt like an empty vessel, that her heart was broken, that she'd packed her bags and stored them at the Beverly Wilshire so her limo driver could swing by the hotel after the show and pick them up on their way to the airport for her red-eye flight back to New York, Caroline Spencer threw herself into her work with her customary focus and determination.

"Her hair should be up," she told Thomas, nodding at one of the models as they stood in the large dressing room amid a maelstrom of seamstresses, makeup artists and hair stylists. "We need to see the high neckline of the dress, not bury it under a pile of curls." The beaded silk gown with the crystal broach was one of the two designs she and Ridge had sparred over when they began their collaboration, the sketch of his that she'd dubbed matronly. She had suggested—and he had conceded—that they should leave the long sleeves and neckline as they were but open up two hip-hugging side panels to create a peek-a-boo look—sexy but still classic and elegant.

"Really glad you caught that," said Thomas, who was trying hard to be his father's eyes for the event and looking a little overwhelmed by it all. "We're very lucky you came back here, Caroline. With you working side by side with Dad, we won't have to worry about the couture line going forward."

Caroline smiled but didn't correct him. No one seemed to know that Ridge had terminated her employment at Forrester Creations. Not Hope, not Donna, not even Pam, who could be absent-minded but kept her ear to the ground for the latest gossip. In fact, Pam had taken Caroline aside in the dressing room earlier, steering her over to a relatively quiet corner.

"I'm sorry your engagement to Rick is off," she'd whispered, as if the information were top secret, as if there really *had* been an engagement. "I happened to hear it on the recorder when I was transcribing Eric's speech, about how you told him there was too much baggage between you and Rick." She'd given herself a hard rap on the head with her knuckles. "I was such a dimwit, leaving that thing at Eric's. I guess I also forgot to hit stop. I hope you don't mind that I listened to everything." She'd sighed. "The battery must have run out so I missed the very end, but from what I heard, you kind of spilled your guts, girlfriend.

"Anyway," said Pam, "I'm sure Rick's disappointed but he kind of made his own bed, so to speak."

"Yes, it's a shame," Caroline had replied in a monotone. "It just wasn't meant to be this time." Her words had sounded hollow, even to her, but they were the best she could do. And she was grateful that Pam left it at that, without even mentioning Ridge. Whether his aunt would keep the information to herself in the long run was out of her control. Caroline squirmed. The thought of Pam dissecting her conversation with Eric that day—her private conversation—was unsettling.

For his part, Rick acted quickly on his disappointment: he brought Maya to the office the day of the fundraiser. Apparently, she was back in LA, and she was suddenly his date for the event. If he intended to rub salt into Caroline's wounds, he didn't succeed—she actually felt relieved at the sight of the two of them together. She had truly loved Rick when they were married, and now she hoped he would find peace and stability in his life. Maybe her high expectations for him hadn't been a source of support but rather a source of pressure and stress and maybe she bore some of the responsibility for the problems in their relationship. Maybe Maya was simply a better fit for him. Maya looked up to him, didn't have aspirations of being his business partner, accepted him for who he was. Maybe it was the two of them who belonged together—a realization that liberated Caroline. What's more, Eric needn't have worried about his sons going to war over her: neither of them wanted her now. The irony wasn't lost on her.

Seeing Ridge at the office was an entirely different story. It wounded Caroline right to her core. Avoiding him was impossible, but she'd made a conscious effort to limit their interactions as much as she could. He'd looked drawn at the meeting he'd scheduled for early that morning with the members of the fundraiser team, his complexion pallid, his speech slow and labored. Had he lain awake all night thinking about her? Replaying what was on the recorder? Regretting his reaction? Wishing she would ignore his edict to leave Forrester Creations, to leave him? Was he as desperate to be with her as she was to be with him, but too proud to admit it? Or had he merely been worried about the fundraiser and how their sneak preview of the couture spring collection would be received? Was it business that kept him tossing and turning, particularly after hearing Eric express his concern about the skittish buyers? She would never know, because he'd dismissed everybody as soon as the meeting was over, including her, and didn't emerge from his office until the preparations for the fashion show were well underway and there wasn't time for anything except getting the models dressed and ready.

It was only after he had changed into his tuxedo minutes before the fundraiser was to begin that she allowed herself to approach him. She had slipped into the same black dress she'd worn at Luc's opening; the symmetry had seemed perfect somehow. Ridge looked dashing in his tux, even with his obvious lassitude, and she decided to tell him so.

"Losing the beard was a good move, and whoever wielded the razor last week knew what they were doing," she said cheerily, as if she didn't have a care in the world.

He smiled ruefully. "Yes, she did." He adjusted his glasses and regarded her. "I'm sure you look pretty great yourself."

"I do, as a matter of fact. You told me so the last time I wore this dress. It's a Forrester Creations original, the black one with the sheer lace bodice. I wore it in New York when your shirt ran into my glass of champagne."

"Well, I'd better find Thomas," he said. "Or let Thomas find me. He's taking me down to the ballroom so I can greet the guests, do the things CEOs do."

"I think the fashion show will be a huge success," she chirped, trying to prolong the conversation for just another moment, clinging to the sliver of hope that she could get him to change his mind and ask her to stay.

"Thanks to you," said Ridge. He reached for her hand, gripping it in a firm, professional-grade handshake and pumping it vigorously, as if he were closing a deal.

"Hey, anytime," she said, her heart sinking with the finality of their parting. "You know ... if you need designs ... or whatever ... feel free to let me know." God, she sounded like some mindless, language-challenged teenager.

There was an awkward silence until a beaming Thomas materialized, the spitting image of his father in an identical tuxedo. "Ready, Dad?"

"Ready, son," said Ridge.

Thomas held his father's elbow as the CEO and his heir apparent headed slowly in the direction of the ballroom.

Don't cry. Don't cry. Don't you dare cry, Caroline admonished herself, watching them walk away, a lump the size of a grapefruit forming in the back of her throat. *If he looks back, even for a split second, it means he still loves you*, she thought, and willed Ridge to do just that, to turn his head so he could catch one last glimpse of her.

She waited, her pulse quickening. *Do it, Ridge. Show me.*

But he didn't. He and Thomas continued down the hall to the ballroom. And then, as if self-correcting an impolite oversight, it was Thomas who glanced back over his shoulder and called out to her with an enthusiastic wave: "Later, Caroline!"

There would be no later, not for her and Ridge, Caroline thought with a heavy sorrow that caused her whole body to slump.

Now, while she monitored every detail of the fashion show from her perch to the left of the stage that had been festooned with flowers, she watched the model wearing Ridge's showstopper, the colorful print gown that was inspired by a trip to the tropics, strut down the runway to close the show to thunderous applause. The designs were a hit without a doubt, and the positive buzz about Forrester Creations would spread all over the internet within the hour. The crowd chanted Ridge's name, demanding that he take a bow, which he did as every single one of the two hundred guests rose to their feet in appreciation. Caroline applauded too, caught up in the moment, her heart swelling with pride for the man who had managed to honor his mother's memory, raise money for a worthy cause and promote his company—all despite his obvious challenges.

Okay, that's enough, Caroline reminded herself. *Time to go home.*

*

"I can't stand places like this," said Gigi as she and Caroline mingled among the other revelers attending the cocktail party. It was the opening of the Wild Boar, a new restaurant that was supposed to be the next hip place for carnivores with either generous corporate expense accounts or healthy trust funds. It was decorated to resemble a hunting lodge with an enormous stone fireplace, tables made out of tree trunks, and walls covered with mounted deer heads. Or were they moose heads? "They should call it the Wild *Bore*. It's like an amusement park without the amusement. Have you ever met such dull people?"

"No," Caroline agreed. The women at the party prattled on about their nanny problems and their gluten sensitivities and their frustration over the congested streets of Manhattan that were making them late for Pilates, acupuncture and yoga. As for the men, they discussed money: how they made theirs and how their wives spent entirely too much of it.

"And when did pig become the new beef?" said Gigi, shaking her head in wonder.

"A few years ago," said Caroline. "You must have missed it while you and your lawyer were negotiating another divorce settlement."

Gigi stuck her tongue out at her friend. Caroline realized she had been peevish all night—peevish since she got back from LA, in fact. "You need another cocktail. Or maybe you'd rather have another saucy sow?" The restaurant's signature appetizer was a slider filled with shredded pork smothered in bourbon sauce, and even Caroline had to laugh when a waiter in a safari outfit and a pith helmet stopped by with a tray of the sows and offered her one.

"No, thanks," she told him, wishing she could just go home and stay there. Attending restaurant openings and art gallery shows and fundraisers to save the unicorns had become tedious. She'd rather spend her nights at the townhouse, parked in front of the television with a glass of wine and her sketchpad.

"Then how about a boar dog?" the waiter suggested, nodding at the tray's other item, a mini hot dog topped with coleslaw. "They're awesome."

"I bet, but I'm really stuffed," she said. "I've been pigging out on your pig all night."

The truth was she hadn't eaten a thing since breakfast. Her appetite was practically non-existent since she'd got back from LA, and she'd dropped more pounds than was becoming.

"You're wasting away," Gigi said as if reading her mind.

Caroline smirked. "Like you should talk. You're a walking carrot stick."

"Yeah, but I've always been this way. You're on some sort of hunger strike and it's ridiculous. Eat something or I'll have to force feed you."

"Actually, *I* was just about to force feed her."

Both women spun in the direction of the male voice that had intruded so rudely on their conversation. Caroline rolled her eyes as she wheeled around to face the interloper, assuming it was yet another husband on the prowl while his wife was off discussing her latest juicing cleanse with her girlfriends.

Arranging a phony smile on her face as she turned, she said, "Thanks anyway, but I'm busy with—"

And then, of course, she saw the male the voice belonged to, let it register in her brain, and she stopped talking—stopped breathing too.

"You have to try their slow-roasted buffalo Reuben on grilled rye," said Ridge, as he chomped on the appetizer-sized sandwich. "The tangy barbecue sauce gives it a nice kick, but it's the melding of the warm Swiss cheese, the Russian dressing and the sauerkraut that creates an intense mouth feel and makes you wonder why anybody would make a Reuben with pastrami. Here, taste."

Before Caroline could protest or shake her head or ask why in the world he was in New York, at the Wild Boar, no less, he was popping the rest of his canapé into her mouth and letting his fingertips trail across her lips. She was so stunned she couldn't even swallow.

"It's good, Caro. I wouldn't steer you wrong," he said. He was grinning like a fool.

"Whatareyoudoinghere?" she said around the mouthful as she started to chew so she wouldn't choke.

"Sorry. I didn't catch that." Ridge laughed. "But if you said buffalo tastes just like chicken, I'll have to disagree. It's velvety and rich like beef but leaner, without all the artery-clogging fat, and it's lower in calories for those of you ladies who watch that sort of thing." He smiled at Gigi. "We haven't met. I'm Ridge Forrester."

"Yes, I know," she said dryly, looking him up and down. "I've heard all about you."

"Only positive things, I hope," he said.

"Not exactly," said Gigi. "You destroyed my friend when you dumped her."

"I didn't dump—" Ridge hesitated. "There's more to it, trust me."

"I hate when guys say, 'Trust me,'" Gigi snapped. "It makes me not trust them. I notice you're not wearing your dark glasses, by the way, and you didn't seem to have any trouble finding Caroline in this crowd. Are you cured of your blindness, or what?"

Caroline gulped down the last of the sandwich, her head swiveling back and forth as if she were at a tennis match while watching the two of them talk, wondering if she should just let them keep at it. Maybe it would be easier to stay quiet and be a spectator. On the other hand, she didn't need a surrogate and she was itching to launch into her own line of interrogation for Ridge Forrester.

"Okay, everybody," she said, washing the food down with the Belgian beer the restaurant was serving. "I'd like a minute with Mr Chowhound. Gigi, would you mind?"

Her friend groaned, either because she didn't want to leave Caroline alone with the guy who'd treated her so shabbily or because there were no interesting men at the party and, therefore, not a single potential target. But after giving Ridge one last dirty look, she made herself scarce.

"So." He gazed at Caroline, his eyes clear and bright and shimmering with love.

"So." Caroline said, echoing him, her lips tingling with the feel of his fingertips, her body buzzing with the memory of his naked body pressed hard against hers that night in his bedroom. Still, the sheer audacity of him showing up on her turf—again—after everything that had happened between them was infuriating.

"I love you, Caro," he said softly, brushing her hair off her shoulder with a gentle caress of his fingers. "I have a lot of explaining to do, but I needed to get that off my chest. I really, really love you."

Her pulse quickened and she felt her legs buckle, but she wasn't about to just collapse into his arms. She wasn't one of his little playthings and she wasn't Brooke, who boomeranged in and out of his life for so many years. "Nice sentiment," she said stiffly, "but I'd rather start with how you knew I'd be here tonight. Or is this a coincidence like the last time? Is the chef another buddy of yours from Paris, someone you met at your favorite café where you were wearing a beret, sipping cognac and listening to Edith Pilaf?"

"It's Pi*af*—if you mean the singer, not the rice."

"Whatever."

"No, no coincidence and no idea who the chef is here. It was Karen who told me where I'd find you. I camped out at your door earlier. Luckily, she didn't slam it in my face."

"My mother has manners, unlike some people." She studied his face and was struck by how at peace he looked now that he was free of the blindness and the accompanying dark glasses and light restrictions. She couldn't help but be elated for him that his sight had returned—or so it seemed.

He took her hands, held them in his. "It turns out that there was more on that recorder, the one Pam left at Dad's house."

"Oh, please. Not the recorder again."

"Rick was determined to keep us apart, so he only played us half of it; the battery did run out but not when he claimed it did. Pam listened to all of what was still there and after waiting and wondering if she should pass it along to me—she was afraid of upsetting me, I guess—she decided I needed to hear it."

"Hear what, for God's sake?" It had been months since she'd had the fateful conversation with Eric. At this point, who could remember what was said and by whom? She was sick about the recorder, sick of dwelling on how an innocent visit with Eric had upended her relationship with Ridge.

"You told my father you loved me unconditionally, that you were in it for the long haul, even if my sight didn't come back."

"I told *you* the same thing at your house." Caroline flashed back to the scene in his library when she'd stated her case but he hadn't believed her, hadn't taken her seriously. "You didn't need the recorder for that."

"I'm talking about Terry Jarvis, Caro." He gripped her hands tighter as if he'd never let them go. "When I heard you tell Eric about him, I realized you were capable of so much more than I gave you credit for, and I'm ashamed of myself, ashamed that I was so filled with self-pity, as you said, that I couldn't see, literally and figuratively. I realized that you're not someone who cuts and runs when the going gets tough, that you hang in there no matter what the obstacles, that you don't view the people you love as a burden just because they need your help, and it humbles me to know you, to learn from you. I had to come here and tell you."

"Oh." Caroline certainly wasn't expecting such a profound and stirring confession, and she was stunned, dumbfounded, her head swimming with the implications. "And your vision?" she asked tentatively. "Is it … ?"

"It's good, really good," he said. "The doctors were right. I just needed to give it time … and patience." He smiled, looking at her with the laser-like focus of the old Ridge, the one she'd run into at Luc's. "Remember all those senses I was always pontificating about? I finally came to mine … about everything."

Acknowledgements

When I moved to LA and was introduced to Rhonda Friedman, supervising producer of The Bold and the Beautiful, we connected in a way only women who are destined to be close friends are connected—i.e. we immediately told each other everything. Since then, we've been each other's champions, personally and professionally. What's more, Rhonda makes a fabulous Thanksgiving turkey and I can't imagine not being at her table for her annual event. I've become a big fan of her show, watching it every afternoon while I take my daily break from writing. When she alerted me that B&B was teaming up with Pan Macmillan Australia for a series of novellas and asked if I'd be interested in writing one even though they weren't my usual genre, I said without hesitation, "You bet I would." So my first thankyou goes to Rhonda for suggesting me to the Pan Macmillan team.

Thanks, too, to Claire Craig of Pan Macmillan, who was not only receptive to my joining her roster of talented authors but offered me the best editorial advice I've ever gotten in my over twenty years of writing novels: "HAVE FUN!" And yes, she used all caps in her email.

Much gratitude to Claire's crew, in-house editors Rebecca Hamilton and Danielle Walker, and freelance editor Kylie Mason, for their outstanding work on this book. They're not only pros but nice people too.

Thanks to Trident Media Group's extremely capable Claire Roberts, Director of Foreign Rights, who helped me make the trans-Pacific leap.

And because *Blindsided by Love* involves a wildfire in California, I must thank Geri Ventura of the Montecito Fire Department, who took the time to help me craft a plausible scenario for Ridge. I had help, too, from Dr Henry Spector, who provided information about flash blindness, the temporary condition from which Ridge suffers.

I could never have written so passionately about the characters from B&B if it weren't for Brad Bell, the genius behind the show who makes daily watching a habit I have no intention of breaking. And bravo to actors Linsey Godfrey, who plays Caroline Spencer, and Thorsten Kaye, who stepped into the role of Ridge Forrester and made the character very much his own. Their portrayals were all the inspiration I needed for this book.

Lastly, thanks to my husband, Michael Forester (no relation to the Forrester clan!), who continues to be amused by the soap opera diva in me.

Made in United States
North Haven, CT
11 November 2024

60156256R00133